I0683106

# Cosmic Contemplations

Charles Clemons

Portal Press

Soddy Daisy
Tennessee

Cosmic Contemplations

Special thanks to Leslie Knight for editorial work and content suggestions.

Published in the United States of America by
Portal Press
9706 Ricole Trail
Soddy Daisy, TN 37379

ISBN 978-0-6151-4287-6

First Printing
February 2007

To my wife Joy, who cares little for weird fiction, but reads every word I write, I love you.

# Table Of Contents

## Stories

## Poem

## Pictures and Artwork

"Not only is the universe stranger than we imagine, it is stranger than we can imagine."

**Sir Arthur Eddington, English astronomer (1882-1944)**

# Intergalactic
# Eden

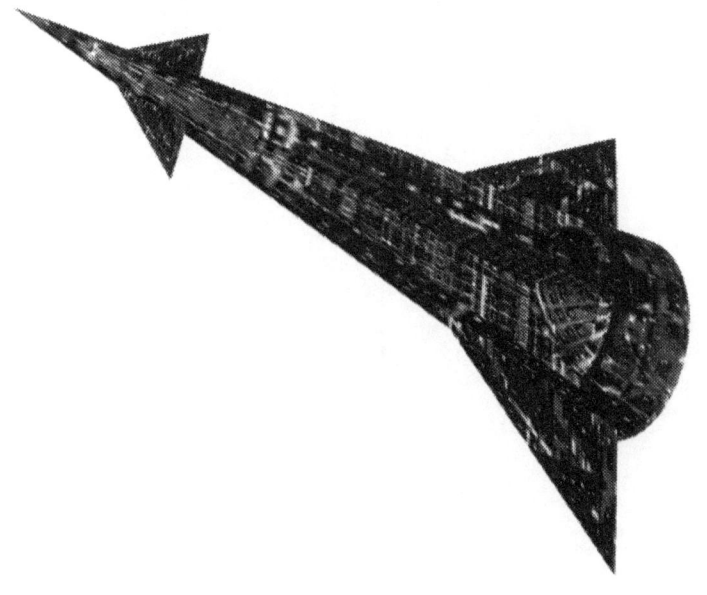

**The Cygnus**

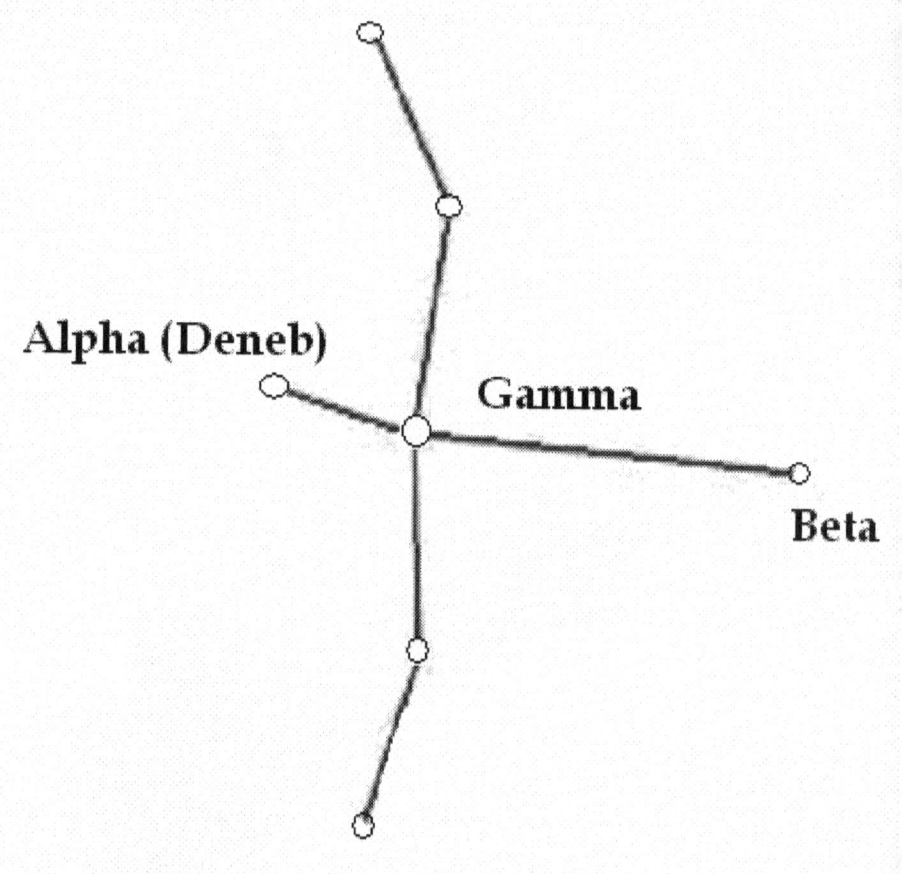

Alpha (Deneb)

Gamma

Beta

# Constellation Cygnus

# Chapter 1

Our ship, The Cygnus, was nothing more than a small freight ship bound for the desolate Deneb solar system and our goal was little more than a new beginning. Thousands of years ago, as Earth crumbled into a slum planet, man became little more than a virus in an expanding universe. Technology had allowed him to spread among planets that once seemed unreachable from his home planet. Man would settle on one planet after another and eventually over populate, exhaust its resources and then move on to repeat the pattern once again. Some of the planets that already had a native people inhabiting it gave resistance, but in the end they always fell to the greed of man. Most of these conflicts repeated themselves, ending historically as discoveries had on our own world, such as the invasion of Earth's western world by the ancient and expanding Europeans. The life forms we found were forced to conform to our culture, moved into galactic reservations or eliminated, as progress always won over sympathy in these matters. I look upon these matters of both our present and past as tragic, but as I write these words, I find myself about to embark on a mission of colonization beyond any in the history of mankind.

Charles Kineard, the leader and founder of our mission, had chosen each of us very carefully. Our group consisted of eight individuals, constituting four couples. The overall mission selections were made based on both our mental and physical attributes, with heavy consideration given to our professions. After all, our children would have to marry each other and genetic flaws could plague or ruin a new civilization.

# Cosmic Contemplations

The first couple, as I like to call them, was Dr. Charles and Mrs. Jane Kineard. Dr. Kineard was a well-known and distinguished scientist considered by most as the utmost authority on planetary physics. He was a tall slender man who always seemed to be in deep thought; even when he was having a conversation, his mind was wandering off elsewhere. Whenever someone spoke with him, they commonly had to repeat themselves to bring him up to par. It was Dr. Kineard who had interviewed and chosen each of us out of the dozens of couples that applied. Dr. Kineard also financed and planned every aspect of his famed genesis mission. His wife Jane, a small woman with red hair and fair skin, was the only one of the expedition that had not endured the interviews and screenings required to accompany the mission. She was also the only one of the group that didn't contribute some type of profession.

The second couple was Sgt. John and Dr. Cynthia Berman. John was an ex-galactic soldier, astronaut and skilled pilot. He was a burly man of tremendous size. His hands, which always seemed to be clinched, looked as if they would have been more at home on a gorilla than on a man. His personality, which matched his physique, was domineering and controlling to say the least. His wife, Dr. Cynthia Berman, was a completely antithetical being compared to her husband. It was not only her profession that made her different, even though she was an established medical doctor with impeccable credentials, it was everything else about her. First of all, her beauty was astounding, not necessarily in a voluptuous sexual manner, as her petite and delicate features radiated an angelic kindness, but quiet and soft like a slow waterfall. Her motions and mannerisms were of a soft and gentle nature.

The third couple, Dr. Edmund and Dr. Jenna Goldstein, were in every way as similar as the Bermans were different. Both were prominent scientists in their fields, he being in botany and she in geology, and both were abnormally bashful. Maybe quiet was a better word, but either way their personalities were far from outgoing. When I first met them, I wondered who had popped the question of marriage between the two and how many years it had taken for such an event. Their appearances left little to describe and while they were not ugly, they were plain.

This brings me to the final couple, my wife and I, Dr. Alex and Dr. Anne Adair. We were the last couple to be chosen due to our late entry. The two of us got married three weeks prior to the launch, but before you get the impression of a young couple blasting off into deep space to live happily ever after, let me explain our situation. Our quick marriage was one of convenience, not love. I had only known Anne for about a week when she made me a proposition that would change our lives forever. Having a doctorate in chemistry, she had been an admirer of Dr. Kineard's work since her early college days, and the chance to work with her greatest mentor was an opportunity that she would not miss. I myself had made the commitment to further my career as a writer and to finish my series of work; *Studies In Alien Nature*. It would consist of three hundred and eighteen volumes, one for each intelligent form of life discovered by man during his explorations. Unfortunately, nine of those races were now extinct and four more were on the brink. Disease, war and loss of habitat were the major culprits, but each race had its own individual story, something I hoped to expose to mankind in my writings. The galactic network was alive with news and reports about Dr. Kineard and his genesis team. My writings had received more exposure since my appointment to Dr. Kineard's team than they could have ever received in any lifetime. It is true that both my degree and practice was in alien psychology, but my first love had always been writing.

Dr. Kineard had spent over three years preparing what would be the most remote space station that man had ever known. Every necessity that a new society could ever require had been secured, including a cold fusion power generator, a hydro extractor, frozen embryos of numerous livestock, a nearly limitless supply of various plant seeds and heavy machinery for construction and cultivation. The station would be built at great expense on a small fertile moon orbiting the immense planet Oniesis. Oniesis itself was nothing more than a volatile ball of swirling gases and violent storms, but our moon Hipparchus II, with help from the heat produced by the gravitational pull of Oniesis, was calm, lush and ideal for colonization.

The trip would be a long one, forty seven years to be exact, but in our cryogenic state, it would seem as only a few hours. The media, local spectators and our families and friends all flocked to the launch site to see us off. My father was composed and supportive of my decision, but my mother, who was almost sixty, was devastated. She continued to remind me that I still had time to change my mind, even as I stood in front of her in my full flight suit. I gave them both a final embrace and walked up the long ramp leading into the belly of our ship, The Cygnus. In all likelihood, they would both be dead before I ever reached the atmosphere of Hipparchus II.

Anne, who had said a brisk goodbye to her family, was already on deck helping Dr. Kineard set our coordinates when I arrived. Her dark brown eyes watched intently as he spoke to her about the details of our coming journey. She was tall for a woman, nearly six feet, but still possessed the thin features of a shorter woman.

Dr. Kineard's wife cared little for the sciences and kept me company during the long delay before lift-off. Her features were fair and her hair was so curly that it barely hung off her head. She was not unattractive, but her personality seemed more like that of an aged grandmother than that of a woman still in her prime. Everything she spoke about seemed out of touch or well beyond the age of her generation. Simply put she was boring, but our conversation was still better than listening to Dr. Kineard and his recital of infinite numbers.

Once all the preliminary details of our trip had been completed, the eight of us sealed our suits and strapped in for take-off. Anne's position was next to mine and she gripped my hand in excitement during the launch, but once we were in space she was back at the side of Dr. Kineard. With her baggy flight suit on and her long golden curls pinned up, you could hardly see her slim elegant physique. It is true I accepted her offer of marriage primarily to advance my own career, but I have to admit that my attraction to her made what would have been a tough decision much easier.

The next three days were spent ensuring that everything would be ready for both our cryogenic sleep and our impending arrival in the Deneb solar system. The slightest miscalculation could send us into the core of some raging star or black hole.

I had been assigned the task of keeping a daily journal to chronicle our voyage. It took up very little of my time as I only wrote between fifteen hundred and two thousand words a day and since a deck full of scientists offered little conversation beyond theories and assumptions, I was able to quietly contribute to my latest book.

The member of the crew with the most colorful idiosyncrasies was Sgt. John Berman. Every other word out of his mouth was synonymous with stereotypes of a bad fictional space pirate or drunken soldier. Some of his comments were innovational clichés that took several minutes for me to grasp their historical meanings and most of his jokes, even though they were often lewd, were hilarious, but I didn't take very well to him. He liked to control every person or thing he came into contact with, even conversations.

On the other hand, John's wife Cynthia was pleasant and easy to talk to whenever you could strike up a conversation with her. She was the only one who seemed to be able to relate to things beyond her profession. However, she would become noticeably uncomfortable whenever she spoke to one of the men of the ship, unless it was her husband or Dr. Kineard.

On the third day I wrapped up my final journal entry and we began the preparation for our long cryogenic sleep. I had traveled by cryogenic sleep before, but never for a period longer than three months. You don't just crawl into your cell, pressurize it and immediately fall asleep. It happens very slowly and before you realize it you're under.

John, not liking to procrastinate, was the first to pressurize and seal his cell. Everyone followed John's lead and within minutes I was the only one who remained awake. I took a few minutes to walk around the ship contemplating my decisions over the past few weeks. Within twenty minutes, the whole ship was in total darkness. I hadn't thought about it, but the ship had been programmed to use as little energy as possible for the next half a century. I stood alone in the dark among the stars and pondered. I hoped that I hadn't made a mistake giving up everyone and everything I knew to volunteer for Dr. Kineard's genesis team. Maybe I had acted too hastily when I had accepted the beautiful Anne's proposal. I kind of got caught up in all the fame and limelight my writings were receiving, as well as her beauty. Just being selected by Dr. Kineard had made me an instant authority in my field, something I had never known and to be honest something I probably would have never known on my own.

I stopped by the ship's main deck and watched its computer silently control every aspect of our journey through space and time. From the observation deck the universe around us slowly glided by. I was immersed in utter black silence. A click from the computer awoke me from my hypnotized state and reminded me of the decision I had made. I decided to delay my long and impending sleep just a little longer and jot down some notes in a personal diary I had kept for several years. My journey of thought finally ended at Anne's cryogenic cell. I looked at her gentle curved lips and soft skin and wondered what the future held for us. I had hoped that once we got away from all the commotion of our impending expedition that we might grow closer, but over the past three days we had done nothing more than speak casually.

I ended my conscious thought by sealing my own cell and closing my eyes. My last thought was not of Anne or even my mother or father, it was of our helpless tiny ship as it plummeted through a strange and endless universe.

# Chapter 2

I had never been in such a long cryogenic state and when I awoke all of my senses except for my hearing were gone. I couldn't see anything through the bright light of our chamber ceiling, which stung my reemerging sight. It took a full five minutes before I was able to walk around and the feeling in my extremities returned. Every tissue in my body, down to the center of my bones, felt as if Novocain surged through my cells.

We were all recovering when Dr. Kineard made an absolutely horrid discovery! Somehow the seal on Mrs. Kineard's chamber cell had cracked! Her respirator had continued to keep her unconscious, but the cool gases in her chamber had lost their pressure and failed to stop her from aging! She had lived a full life and died of old age without ever knowing!

Upon the return of our olfactory senses, our entire group succumbed to the uncontrollable gagging stench radiating from her cell. From the look of her decayed body, she appeared to have been dead for at least a year. Being a man of rationalization, Dr. Kineard showed little emotion and had even come up with a theory on what had happened within minutes of the discovery. Dr. Jenna Goldstein went into hysteria and fell to the floor in a blubbering mass.

"What are we going to do?" sobbed Jenna wildly.

Her husband stumbled over to her and held her face to his chest covering the hideous scene. "Calm down now Jenna, everything is going to be all right," he said in a soothing tone.

"We can't continue now," screamed Jenna while gripping onto her husband's cryogenic suit with all her might, "not without Jane!"

She began to heave and vomit from extreme nausea, brought on by the stress of witnessing such a horrifying sight. After regaining most of my strength, Edmund and I carried her out of the room. I helped him get her to their living quarters then went back up to the cryogenic chamber to locate Cynthia. When I got there, I found Dr. Kineard, Anne, John and Cynthia discussing our situation. Anne was standing so close to Dr. Kineard that it would have been hard to squeeze a beam of light between their bodies.

"When do you want to do it?" asked John.

"Cynthia," I interrupted, "I think Edmund is going to need your help calming Jenna down."

Cynthia placed her little hand against her cheek. "Oh, what was I thinking? Of course he does," she said in alarm.

I watched her quickly leave the room before I turned to look at the remaining three members of our expedition.

"When do we want to do what?" I asked.

"We were talking about what we were going to do," answered John.

"And just what are we going to do?" I asked.

"We are going to have a proper funeral and continue on the best that we can," Dr. Kineard answered nonchalantly.

"You can't be serious!" I replied in shock. "Surely you don't expect us to carry on as if nothing has happened!"

"I never meant anything of the sort," said Dr. Kineard as calmly as if he was in a debate. "I only meant that since we can't change the current situation, we should move on and deal with the ones that we can."

"I don't remember discussing our situation at all!" I yelled.

"We are not going to turn back if that is what you mean!" boasted John.

"I volunteered to join this group. I wasn't drafted and I don't like people making decisions for me without my consent," I declared looking up into his face.

He scoffed at me and turned around as if my defiance of him was nothing but a joke. Acting out of rage instead of reason, I shoved him as he turned and caused him to trip on his own feet. I could see the anger boil from within him as he jumped up and if it weren't for Anne between the two of us, he probably would have pounded me into the floor below.

"Dr. Adair, please calm down! I assure you that we were going to consult with you on this, we were just conferring on a reasonable course of action," responded Dr. Kineard.

"As I see it, we have two reasonable choices," I said.

"I know you don't think turning back would be in our best interest. We have all sacrificed too much to give up now. Besides, what would we go back to? By the time we got back almost a hundred years would have passed and no one we know would still be alive. After what has happened, do you want to seal yourself back up in one of those chambers for fifty years and hope for the best?" said Dr. Kineard.

I didn't answer him, for I knew he was right. If I had made the wrong decision in coming it was too late to change it now. Dr. Kineard looked at me for a moment and then asked John to check our coordinates. He grudgingly agreed and watched me through the corner of his eye as he slowly left the room. Anne beamed with pride whenever her mentor spoke and his victorious debate with me made her light up like a star. If he were leading us into a black hole it seemed she would go in with him with that very same smile.

We held Mrs. Kineard's funeral early the next morning and gave our last respects before blasting her remains off into space. Jenna felt much better once she came to terms with the situation and even helped plan our landing later that evening.

The next five days, before our landing on Hipparchus II, consisted of nothing but constant planning and preparation. John spent most of his time in the hull prepping both our landing equipment and building materials, while Dr. Kineard, Anne, and Jenna debated on the best landing site. I returned to my writing, primarily out of boredom, and had just finished another chapter in my book, when Edmund knocked on my door.

His voice muffled through the door, "Dr. Adair, Dr. Kineard has called a meeting in the bridge."

I took only a few minutes to change my clothes before I left for the bridge. When I got there everyone else was already seated and in deep debate.

"Please Dr. Adair, join in," said Dr. Kineard while pointing towards an empty chair.

After I sat down he continued, "I asked everyone here to discuss the future of this expedition. After speaking with Alex earlier, it has come to my attention that we need to set up a few rules to help govern our new civilization. From now on, all major decisions will be voted upon, with each member of our society having a single vote. Any member of the group can submit an idea for vote and majority will rule. There will be no form of representative government here, as everyone will have his or her own say in every matter. With the level of education in this room, I think this simple form of constitution will work the best."

The first vote on the agenda was the location of our landing and future site of our base. Dr. Kineard favored a valley that was surrounded on three sides by two different mountain chains. He believed that it would offer substantial protection from the weather and other natural catastrophes. Jenna on the other hand, thought that since it was so close to mountains that the soil would be rocky and offer poor agriculture possibilities. She favored a location further to the south near a large series of lakes. Edmund agreed with his wife, mentioning that the mountains of Dr. Kineard's landing site, dubbed site A, might act as barriers and make it difficult to reach necessary resources. John looked at the situation purely from a military standpoint and liked the defensive location of site A. After a short debate, Dr. Kineard opened the floor to a vote. Dr. Kineard, Anne, and John all voted for Dr. Kineard's protective site A, while Jenna, Edmund, Cynthia and I all voted for Jenna's more fertile site B. Anne's brown eyes focused on me as I made my vote public and then turned away at its conclusion. When she returned to our quarters that night, she went straight to bed without speaking.

The next morning when I awoke she was already gone. I went above to the galley and ate breakfast with John, Cynthia, Jenna and Edmund. During the meal, I found out that Anne and Dr. Kineard were working on launching Corvus, a satellite that would orbit our new world and offer us a bird's eye view of Hipparchus II's surface. John's mouth widened into a smile when he discovered that I had been oblivious to Anne's whereabouts, but a quick glance from Cynthia returned it to his previous apathetic state.

I excused myself after finishing breakfast and went above to the bridge to observe our tiny moon. It was little more than a bright green ball orbiting around the fiery red gases of the great mass Oniesis. We had already received several transmissions from a land probe sent to the surface three days ago and what we saw had surpassed all of our expectations. The surface was covered in thick virgin forest, deep blue lakes and white peaked mountains, all free from the touch of man. We scheduled the landing of our ship near site B for early the next morning, with the plan being to set up our base and never leave the moon's surface again.

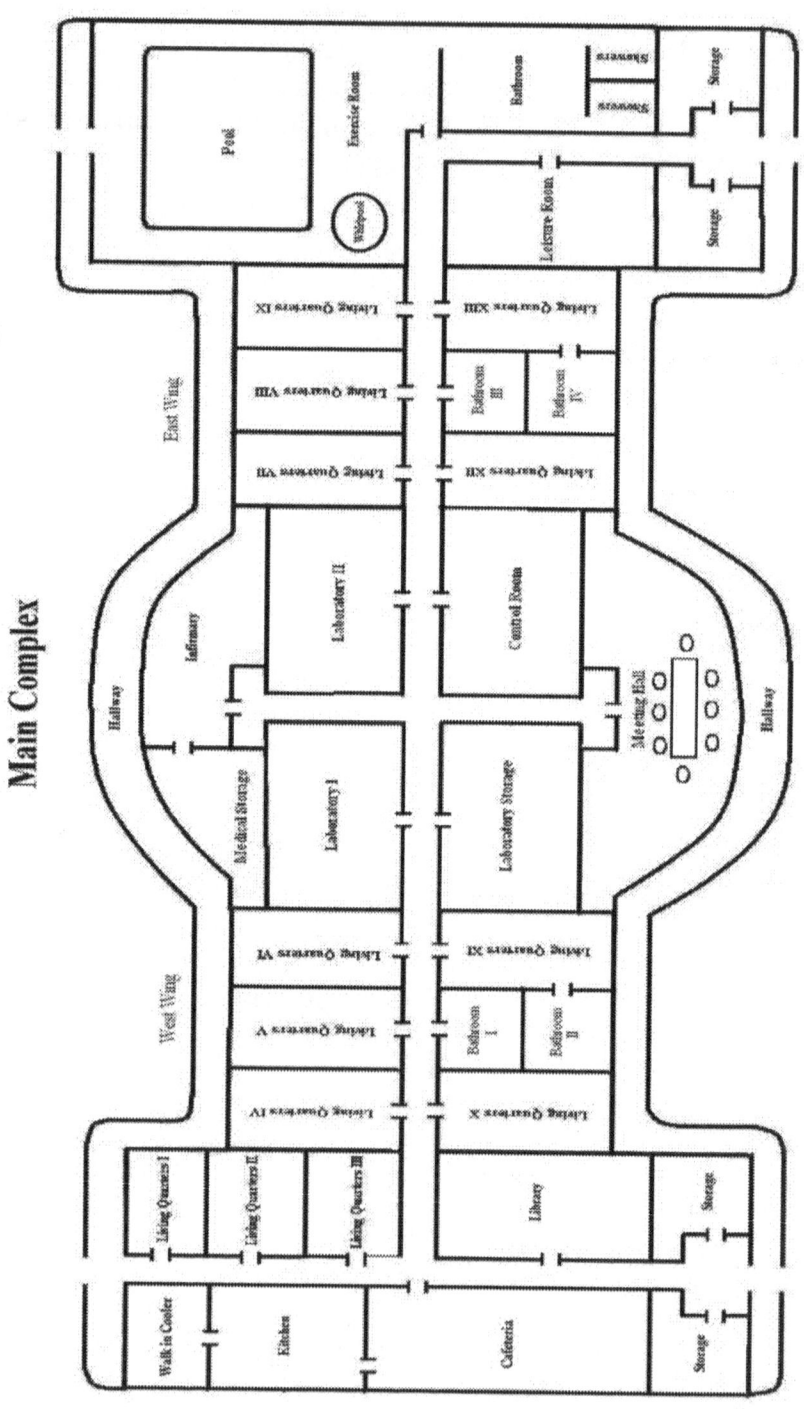

# Chapter 3

Our landing went as planned, and except for Dr. Kineard's ceremony of taking the first step on Hipparchus II, it was a pleasant one. Anne was the second to step on its soil following in the footsteps of Dr. Kineard like a lost puppy. Edmund displayed the excitement of a child at Christmas running from one plant to another examining their every detail. I have always considered myself to be a man of composure, but I myself was at a loss of words. It was a scene of absolute beauty. All around the small clearing of our landing zone was the splendor of nature untouched by the hand of man. It was a moment of sensual delight. Every one of our senses reached their peak of stimulation. A soft cool breeze rolled across my skin carrying the scent of bloom to caress my olfactory senses, while the gentle sound of nature was as pleasant of an auditory sensation as any I had ever heard. Before us was Jenna's Lake, as it would later be named, stretching out in a flat blue plane as far as the naked eye could see.

A feeling of pride came over me, even though I had nothing to do with its creation and little to do with its discovery. It was the type of pride that must have filled the hearts of the eastern men who discovered the western world of Earth. This was now our world, no one else's.

After storing our abandoned space ship in a vacuumed sealed plastic-type bag, we spent the next two months constructing what would not only be our home, but the future home of our children and grandchildren. Our newly created colony consisted of four major buildings. The first, our main complex, was by far the largest and most extensive. It was designed around one main chamber, which broke off into two separate wings. In all it consisted of thirty-five rooms, broken down into thirteen sleeping quarters, one cafeteria, five full bathrooms, an exercise room, a library, an indoor pool, four storage rooms, two laboratories, an infirmary, a leisure room, a kitchen, a walk in cooler, a control room, a meeting hall, a medical storage and laboratory storage room. The second building was a large warehouse, while the third and fourth buildings were a barn and greenhouse. The entire compound's boundaries were determined by a thick seven foot tall metallic fence that could be energized for security reasons, which completely encircled the four aforementioned buildings, numerous gardens, livestock corrals, a cold fusion unit and a hydro-atmospheric extractor. All of our power derived from a small simple cold fusion unit, which did nothing more than create fusion between two deuterium nuclei of helium and then harness its power. While taking up only a space measuring four feet by four feet, it was capable of supplying enough power to support a community a hundred times our size! Our hydro-atmospheric extractor was the most technically advanced available on the market at the time of our departure and was capable of extracting both molecules of hydrogen and oxygen and bonding them together to form water in even the most arid of atmospheres.

Using heavy equipment, John did most of the heavy labor while the rest of us divided into teams and worked on the final touches of each individual building. Edmund and I spent most of two months working together on his greenhouse and developing a close kinship. Once I got to know him better, his shy demeanor quickly faded and I found him to be very intelligent and quite interesting. He had a love for his work that took him beyond the stuffy doors of his lab carrying him into the open fields that harvested his interest. He took a nature walk every day and several times we went out on overnight trips collecting samples for his work. In just over a month, he had identified and classified over six hundred new species of plants. We also had brought several strains of our own plants, but Edmond would not approve their transplant until he, his wife, Anne and Dr. Kineard had finished checking the soil content and the possible effects that alien plants could have upon the immediate habitat.

# Intergalactic Eden

Anne spent most of her time helping Dr. Kineard with comprehensive research on the chemical makeup of our surrounding soil, air and water. I have to admit that I developed internal manifestations of anger and jealously toward her relationship with her mentor, Dr. Kineard, which intensified with every failure I encountered in the growth of our personal relationship. She continued to stay in the same sleeping quarters as I, but spent the rest of her time assisting Dr. Kineard in his work, which translated into ten hour days, six days a week. Our conversations continued to be colorless and she only showed enthusiasm toward me when I allowed her to talk about her work with Dr. Kineard. It wasn't really her fault, as she had never promised the prospect of anything more than a professional relationship from the beginning. My disappointment yielded solely from my secret desire for it to be far more. Officially, we had been married for forty seven years but we still spoke as nothing more than acquaintances. She had given up everything to work with the great Dr. Kineard and being a man of reason, I couldn't rightly stand in her way. Instead, I spent my time with Edmund tending to his plants during the day and alone in my quarters writing at night.

My relationship with John had not improved since I had foolishly pushed him on board The Cygnus. I offered to help him once when he was building our barn, but he greeted me with silence and looked away, continuing on with his work as if I didn't exist. During the next the three months, our pride built and maintained a wall of silence between the two of us.

My relationship with his wife, Cynthia, was a different matter. She was petite, being barely five foot two, and probably didn't weigh much over a hundred pounds. I still sniggered under my breath when I saw her next to John who towered above her at six and a half feet and probably weighed somewhere around two hundred and fifty pounds. They were a classic case of "opposites attract". At first, she gave each one of us a physical once a week, but scaled it down to once a month once she was sure that our new environment had no immediate adverse affects. As I had mentioned earlier, she was the only member of our group who could escape from her profession once she walked away from it. She was very athletic and loved to swim in our indoor pool, which she did about twice a day: once in the afternoon and once in the evening before she went to bed. After the first couple of months, she began to break away from her shyness with me and the only person I spoke with more was Edmund.

Having very little in common with his own wife, John spent most of his days either hunting, at which he was excellent as his game served as the main course for many meals, or tending to our livestock. Being a Psychiatrist, I knew that the unhealthy infatuation I had toward Cynthia probably came from the stress associated with the emotional inadequacies of my own marriage, but to understand the problem and to cure it were two totally different phenomena. Eventually, I found myself going to take swims because I knew she was going to be there. One afternoon my fixation for her almost went too far. I had gotten to the pool a little earlier than usual and was already taking a relaxing swim when Cynthia arrived. She was as punctual as always and when she saw me, her soft red lips gave way to a pleasant smile. I waved at her and continued to swim pretending to not pay her much attention. She put her long black hair up, so it would not get wet, and slipped off her robe. After taking off her sandals, she gracefully slipped into the pool barely creating a ripple. Her lithe body glided through the water effortlessly and rested next to mine. There was always a thick tension between the two of us whenever we first met, but after a few minutes of general conversation it drifted away and we began to enjoy each other's company. I couldn't quite place it, but Cynthia's beauty was somehow different from Anne's. Anne's was more of a physical beauty that was clearly evident to everyone at first sight, but Cynthia's was more of a serene beauty. It was slow and quiet and it continued to grow each time you met her as if it had no limitations. I scarcely remember a word she said during the conversation we had over the next ten minutes, but I do remember unconsciously reaching out and gently touching her arm. She didn't pull her arm away but continued on with her conversation as if my hand was not unwelcome. Suddenly the door to the poolroom slung open and Edmund came in! The noise of the door slamming against the wall startled both of us and I instinctively pulled my hand back as quickly as I had put it out. Although I had touched her, I wasn't really sure if she had noticed. Edmund's face was gripped with distress and my heart nearly jumped out of my chest when I thought of what he might have seen, but what he said made me forget about the entire encounter.

"We've spotted an alien!" he yelled.

When I got outside, I found Anne, Jenna and Dr. Kineard at the edge of our compound's eastern gate staring out toward Jenna's Lake. Dr. Kineard was looking eagerly through a pair of scoptic binoculars.

"It doesn't appear to be carrying any weapons or for that matter, any objects of any kind," he reported.

"Does it appear to be intelligent?" asked Anne anxiously.

"It is walking on two legs but I can't seem to find anything on its body to make a concrete determination either way," he replied.

Edmund stepped up beside me, put his hand on my shoulder and peered out toward the open field between our compound and Jenna's Lake.

"Can you see him Alex?" he asked me.

I shook my head in silent answer and continued to stare in the direction Dr. Kineard had been pointing, but was unable to see anything in the distance. I suddenly realized that everyone from our group was huddled together, except for John. I quickly looked around the compound and was about to inquire as to his whereabouts when I spotted his form. He was lying prone on the roof of our barn staring out toward the object of our curiosity the only difference was that his eye was observing it through the cross hairs of a riflescope!

# Cosmic Contemplations

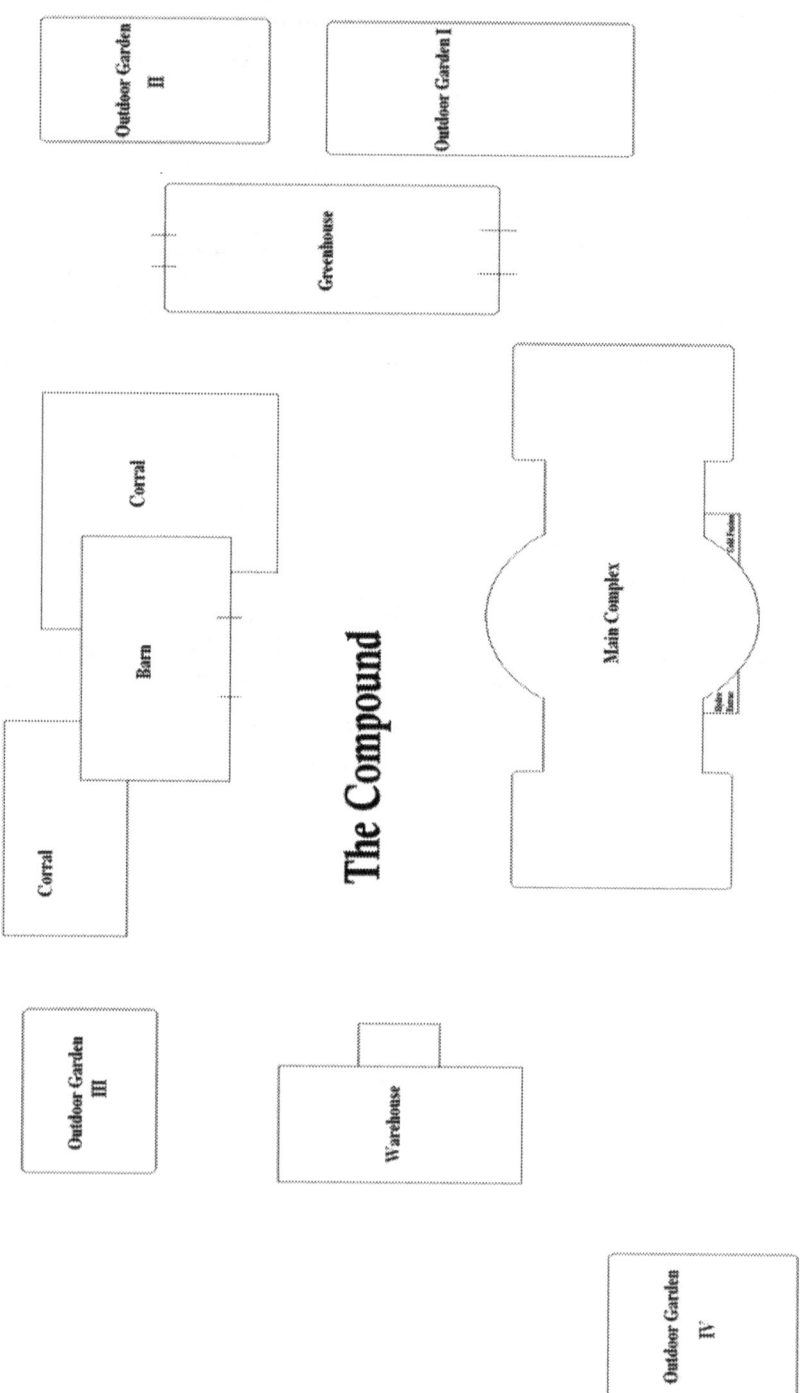

# Chapter 4

I finally got my turn to look through Dr. Kineard's binoculars and see our newest neighbor for the first time. He wasn't tall by our standards, about five and a half feet, and as Dr. Kineard had mentioned, he wore absolutely nothing. He was slender and had an endoskeleton covered with skin of a dark golden-brown. His facial features were flat with nothing protruding, not even ears or a nose. From the best I could tell, his cranium looked to be about the same size as our own but more rounded and his eyes appeared to be very small in proportion to his large face.

"What should we do?" asked Jenna with a puzzled face.

"I don't think we have enough information to do anything at the present," answered Dr. Kineard, "for now all we can do is wait."

"I'll tell you one thing we can do," I said looking in the direction of John, "we cannot point weapons at it until it gives us a reason to do so."

"I am the one who asked John to take a defensive position until we know for sure that it doesn't have malicious intentions," Dr. Kineard replied officiously.

"What if John's perception of malicious intent is different than this creature's?" I retorted smartly. "I want our colonization on this planet to be one of peaceful integration not one of murder and conquest."

"As do we all Dr. Adair, but this new discovery of possible intelligent life has changed everything. Now not only do we have to concern ourselves about our own physical safety, but we also have to be concerned about a totally new and unknown life force," said Dr. Kineard.

Dr. Kineard returned to the magnification of his binoculars and continued to observe our latest discovery on the surface of Hipparchus II.

"Besides we will all know in a matter of moments. He..." Dr. Kineard paused for a moment to mentally grasp a more appropriate word and continued, "it's heading directly for our compound."

Less than half an hour passed before it was standing in the middle of our compound. The six of us stood in awe of the unusual creature. Dr. Kineard had positioned himself several feet ahead of the rest of us and stood ready to greet our surprise visitor. The way we stood, without a motion or sound, must have made us look like a welcoming party greeting a long lost war hero thought to be dead. It looked at us curiously silent as even its feet did not make a sound against the rough soil upon entering our compound. From up close, I was able to better study its features and what interested me the most was its skin. As I had mentioned earlier, it was a dark golden brown but its texture was closer to that of leather than our soft intergumentary tissue. After several uncomfortable moments of silence and stares, Dr. Kineard spoke. The word hello had just passed his lips when our visitor raised its arms up over its face and jumped back seemingly alarmed. The abrupt action startled all of us and froze Dr. Kineard's lips in mid-sentence. I looked up at our barn and after seeing John, I felt more comfortable. The alien slowly lowered its hands in front of its body and focused on Dr. Kineard's mouth. It touched its own as if to understand what he had done and then pointed directly to Dr. Kineard's. Dr. Kineard spoke once again and the creature jumped back as it did earlier but this time not in such a dramatic manner. Dr. Kineard continued to speak in a low tone and we watched as it turned its head from side to side to observe the movement of his lips. Then to all of our amazement, it began to walk toward Dr. Kineard and from the frantic expression on Jenna's face, I began to fear that she might faint or even worse, scream. Dr. Kineard stood his ground and continued to talk in a soft tone until it slowly and gently touched his lips! Its finger muffled his words and Dr. Kineard stopped speaking. Then, to add to our astonishment, the being began to hum! At first I thought that it was trying to mimic Dr. Kineard, but after a few moments I could hear distinct starts and stops in its humming and copious pitches. It was attempting to communicate with us! It continued to hum to Dr. Kineard and all the while its mouth never moved. Then all of a sudden, it stopped. Dr. Kineard began to talk again but this time it ignored him and turned its attention toward Edmund's outdoor garden number three. The gardens he kept outside were native plants and apparently it recognized them. Continuing to ignore us, it walked past our bewildered group and began to pull plants out of the soil by their stalks and stuff them into its mouth. It stopped eating only long enough to turn its head to see if we approved of its actions and upon seeing we were not upset, preceded to pick more. We stood motionless until it left the gates of our perimeter and headed across the great field from which it came. Once it was out of the range of our scoptic binoculars, we held an emergency meeting.

Dr. Kineard continued to treat every action as if we were some newfound country and insisted I keep record of every act so future generations could both cherish and reference them. He then opened the floor to what would be recorded as our first emergency meeting.

"It appears we have made another remarkable discovery," he said in a light tone, "now all we have to do is determine what to do about it."

"I didn't like it!" exclaimed Jenna in obvious distress. "Its enigmatic humming gave me an uneasy feeling."

"It didn't appear to exhibit any patterns of violence," replied Edmund.

"We can't afford to take any chances," John said while leaning back in his chair, "I say we assume the worst and then at least we will be prepared."

"If we assume the worst, then we are not giving this poor creature a fair chance," I rebutted.

"It barged in here and took our food without asking!" screamed John.

"What it did may be part of some custom unfamiliar to us or it might have just been in a state of malnutrition. You have to remember this was his world long before ours and we are the invaders here, not him. To judge this being's actions by our standards is not fair to him or us," I said.

"Just what do you want us to do Alex, sit here with our thumbs up our butt and let him take everything that is ours because he was here first?" asked John sarcastically.

"I doubt there would be room in yours for your head," I said shrewdly.

I regretted saying every single word in that sentence the very moment they passed my lips. John jumped up from his seat and it went sprawling to the floor behind crashing against the wall. If it had not been for Cynthia's arm, I believe he would have come across the table. Dr. Kineard stood up to restore order.

"Please, let's not be counterproductive and return to the situation at hand," he said firmly.

After another hour and half, the meeting came to close with little progress. The only thing we all agreed was that we needed to know more. However, a unanimous vote was made to increase our security and a schedule was made for one of us to be on guard around the clock. Most of us made some type of slight change to our daily routine and no one was allowed outside the complex alone. Edmund and I refrained from taking our usual overnight trips and John, since he didn't have a hunting partner, refrained from hunting altogether. The only two people who didn't change their daily patterns were my wife and Dr. Kineard. Their days continued to be spent analyzing Hipparchus II from within the walls of their lab.

The tension between John and I had grown to such an extreme level, after our last meeting, that it began to make our whole community a little uneasy. Cynthia ceased her swimming sessions altogether and John stopped eating in the cafeteria during normal eating times. I continued to swim twice a day even though I had to do so in solitude, as some of her love for it had manifested itself in me.

It had been a long day and Edmund and I had spent most of it planting a new fruit tree that was indigenous only to the planet Beloin. Even with the extensive knowledge of modern day science, it had never produced a single virere outside its natural habitation. The viere tree, when in full bloom, produced a lush and sweet fruit that was almost neon green and carried the very same name. It was one of those unexplainable mysteries of science, according to paper it was feasible, but once it was taken outside the lab and attempted in a natural setting it failed. We crossed our fingers with every seed we planted and hoped to be able one day to pick vireres with our own hands.

After finishing a cup of coffee with Edmund and Jenna, I returned to my quarters so to get some rest for my pending late night guard shift. When I got to my room I found Anne lying on the bed reading a book. When she saw me, she asked me how my day had gone as if nothing at all was wrong between the two of us.

"Fine," I replied, "how is your work with Dr. Kineard going?"

"I wasn't feeling very well today and Charles insisted that I take the day off. He wouldn't hear of anything else," she said twirling her hair with one hand and holding her book with the other, all the while her eyes never left the pages of her book.

"Did you let Dr. Berman know?" I asked inquisitively.

"Yeah, but she said it was just a cold and not to worry about it."

"Never the less, maybe you should take off tomorrow," I said. "I know this wonderful spot that Edmund and I found. It's near a waterfall and I thought that maybe we could take a picnic."

"No, I just couldn't. Charles and I are in the middle of a possible breakthrough! I only took off today to satisfy his concern. He'll have difficulty completing the experiments without me," she said interrupting me emphatically.

"I just thought since we hadn't spent much time together, we could at least try and spend one day together every once in a while."

"What do you mean? We sleep in the same bed almost every night. You have your aspirations and I have mine. Besides it's what we came here to do."

"I know, but surely we can afford to take some leisure time!" I responded.

Anne put down her book and looked into my eyes for the first time in months. "Listen," she said, "I didn't give up my life and travel billions of miles to take picnics by a waterfall! I came here for the opportunity to work alongside the great Dr. Kineard and make discoveries beyond anyone in my field, past or present. If you want to waste your time frolicking around like some damn fool that's fine by me! Just leave me out of it."

Afraid of what I might say, I stormed out of the room without saying word. When it came time for my shift, John found me asleep in the leisure room and handed me his rifle without saying a word.

Sitting up in the dark, I wondered how I had managed to upset so many people in such a short period of time. Sure, I had earned John's silence by provoking him, but the avoidance I received from both Anne and Cynthia didn't seem wholly fair. I would be fooling myself if I didn't accept most of the blame, but I also believe that the environment I had been introduced into was a major contributing factor. I had come here under false pretenses, fabricated by my own unrealistic expectations about my relationship with the beautiful Anne.

I took my post on top of our barn and sat down to wait out the next four hours. John had built something similar to what used to be called a crow's nest perched high upon our barn. It was small but did allow us to sit down on a flat surface instead of the slanted roof of our barn. I sat in the cold darkness holding my rifle and contemplating my relationship with each member of our society when a long continuous tone broke my concentration. Being careful not to make any noise, I began to strain both my senses of sight and hearing in hopes of locating the tone's origin. It started and stopped several times and seemed to come from several places in unison. Using my night vision scope, I began to scan the field that lead up to our compound and what I caught within my sight, nearly froze my heart! The sound I had been hearing was various tones of hums coming from not one of our newly discovered aliens, but dozens of them! They moved with the speed of insects and seemed to glide across the ground with only the tips of their toes touching its surface. I sat as still as my body would allow and watched them approach our compound in terror. They effortlessly slipped their slender bodies through the small thin space between the poles in our energized fence without even grazing it and began to raid our outdoor gardens. They fought like savages and tore food not only from the ground, but also from the arms of each other. They acted like greedy children as even with food in their hands and mouths full, they struggled for more. Their constant bickering and barbaric stuffing of their grubby little faces not only disgusted me, but also horrified me. From what I observed, reasoning with them would be near hopeless. Not having the heart to kill one of them, I directed a long energy burst into the air and sent the lot of them scurrying back from whence they came. My blast brought to light the condition of our compound and the newfound seriousness of our situation.

# Chapter 5

The seven of us sat down in our little meeting room for what would be our fourth official meeting. As soon as Dr. Kineard opened the floor for discussion, Jenna went into a delirium.

"Did you see what they did to our outdoor gardens?" she yelled shaking. "If someone had not been there to scare them away, they might have gotten in here while we were sleeping!"

"I would like to submit a vote to send a party to find out where they live and put an end to this whole thing right now," said John emphatically.

"Do you mean hunt them down and kill them?" asked Edmund while trying to console Jenna.

"Yes," he answered, "that is exactly what I mean."

His response shocked everyone, even his own wife whose face distorted as if she had been smacked by his words.

"These things," he continued, "have destroyed all of our outdoor food sources. They have pushed us into a survival of the fittest and I assure you I won't allow these things to starve us!"

"I don't think we should take such drastic measures against these beings yet," I retorted, not daring to let anyone know how I had seen them act, "at least until we take more time to learn about their culture."

"Listen," said John standing up in a fury, "I'm getting sick and tired of all you damn scientist wanting to dissect and analyze everything! This is not a lab experiment that we are talking about, this is our life!"

"Yes I know," I responded in a fury of my own, "but we are also civilized human beings with the ability to reason. If we don't make every possible attempt to coexist peacefully with these native beings then we are nothing more than savage animals."

After several minutes of debate, Dr. Kineard stood up to ease the tension around the table and opened the floor to a vote.

"All in favor of Mr. Berman's proposal say aye," he said.

Both John and Jenna responded. Edmund nearly twisted his neck turning to look at his wife when he heard her surprising response. After recognizing their votes, Dr. Kineard then opened the floor for my proposal.

"All in favor of Dr. Adair's proposal say aye," he said again.

The remainder of our panel sided with me, causing John to leave the meeting in disgust. The meeting continued on for another hour, without John's presence, before we finally adjourned.

Three major courses of action were decided upon. First that we should increase the defenses of our compound, second that we should stay on constant alert, and finally that a party should be sent out to observe our neighbors in their native habitat.

The only part of the meeting that didn't go as I had hoped was the selection of the observation party as Dr. Kineard selected John and I. I had been selected for my knowledge of alien behavior and John for his skills in soldiery.

After the meeting I took the time to go and see Dr. Kineard. He was in his lab with Anne, as usual, working on some soil samples. Looking through the frosted glass in the door, I saw the two working together silently. Standing next to her mentor, she worked diligently and was as content as I had ever seen her in the short time I had known her. I am ashamed to admit that seeing her so happy with him mad me angry.

"Dr. Kineard, I would like with talk with you about something," I said through the door after knocking.

"Please come in," he said without looking up from his microscope.

I gently opened the door and stepped into the lab. It was much longer than wide and in its center were two long tables lined side by side which were covered with extensive research equipment. The lab's perimeter was covered by wall-to-wall glass cabinets that were filled with samples from Hipparchus II's surface. Anne turned to look at me curiously, but Dr. Kineard's eye never left its perch high atop his microscope.

"Yes Dr. Adair," he said quickly, "you wanted to talk?"

"I would like to speak with you privately, if possible," I said loudly enough for Anne to hear.

"That all depends on your wife," he said cutely.

Taking his cue, Anne excused herself and closed the door behind her.

"Dr. Kineard," I said, "I'm concerned about the observation party leaving tomorrow morning."

"If I'm not mistaken, this was mostly your idea," he said while moving his slide back and forth.

"I'm not sure that John should be allowed to go, considering his position on the Aluta."

He stopped playing with his slide and looked up at me queerly.

"Aluta?" he asked inquisitively.

"That is what I have named them."

"Interesting name," he said pondering for a moment, before continuing on with the subject at hand. "But as you mentioned earlier, we are civilized beings and John will act within the will of the group, even if he doesn't agree."

"I am not so sure," I said quickly.

"He has done nothing to undermine our faith in him," he said, "and I do believe that he deserves that same chance that we are giving your Alutas, besides his skills in soldiery might prove useful on a hostile or otherwise unexplored planet."

Realizing what he said about John was right I agreed with him and went back to my quarters to get ready for our excursion the next morning. I passed Anne in the hall but neither of us spoke. That night I started volume three nineteen in my volume of works, *Studies in Alien Nature, Volume Three Nineteen, The Aluta.*

I tossed and turned in my bed all night and awoke the next morning feeling tense and uneasy about my pending expedition with John. Everyone was up early and walked with us to the main gate to say goodbye. John, as always, was armed to the teeth, carrying an energy rifle, a knife, a machete and an energy pistol. The only weapon I chose to bring was an old metallic powder pistol. As most old weapons, it was loud, and I assumed from my previous experience that the noise it made when fired would send any Alutas running.

We weren't sure how long we would be gone, or if we would even be able to find the creatures again, but in any matter our packs carried enough supplies to last both of us two full weeks. I said goodbye to everyone, but sadly the only true one was with my good friends, Edmund and his wife Jenna. Edmund gripped my hand in his and hugged me with his other arm, while Jenna hugged me with genuine concern, unlike Cynthia who ignored me through admiration of her husband. Anne kissed me on the cheek but she might as well have shaken my hand. He lips were as cold and lifeless as a piece of ice. Dr. Kineard spoke to us with the tone of a politician saying things that lacked any real emotion in the monotone of an over-rehearsed speech. Not being big on goodbyes, John held still just long enough for Dr. Kineard to finish his speech before he began his hike toward Jenna's Lake. Knowing absolutely nothing of tracking and very little of hunting, I threw my supplies over my back and began following his lead, glad to get away from Dr. Kineard's incessant dribbling. Trying to ease the tension between the two of us, I began to ask John questions about subjects that I thought he would find interesting, but I got no response from him save an occasional yes or no. Finally, after several failed attempts on my part to strike up a conversation, he stopped and turned around.

"I know what you are trying to do," he said sighing, "and I appreciate it, but the first rule of hunting is to shut your trap. With all the noise you are making we would have a hard time tracking down a drunken sloth in a wheelchair."

Then without waiting for a response he turned around and continued following the trail of the Alutas through the dense trees of Hipparchus II. His comment, although correct and probably meant with the best of intentions, infuriated me and the two of us didn't talk the rest of the day.

That night we set up camp near a bay on Jenna's Lake and lit a small fire for security. John had acquired the bad habit of smoking an ancient Earth strain plant called Nicotiana and, thanks to the efforts of Edmund he had plenty of it to smoke. It had lost its popularity nearly a millennium ago when man began to colonize other planets and found space and soil too precious to waste on a plant with no practical nutritional or medicinal value. The cost of growing and shipping made it such a luxury that it eventually became scarce and relatively unknown. I had never seen or smelled it until I saw John smoking it several months ago, and after inquiring of Edmund about it, he gave me some. It burned my eyes, throat and nose and stunk, yet here was John inhaling it in front of me as if it was as smooth as silk.

"About earlier," he said letting out a puff of smoke, "I'm sorry about the sloth in a wheelchair comment. You brainy types kind of get me uptight, you know, and in case you didn't notice, I'm the only one here who is not a doctor."

"It's all right," I said laughing a little. "It's kind of funny when you think about it."

We both had a laugh and I believe that the wall between us cracked just a little. Not enough to see through, but enough to know that it wasn't completely impenetrable.

The next morning we woke up and left our camp between the risings of Hipparchus II's dual suns. It was a damp day, as were most on our fertile little moon, and everything we had was wet. I had difficulty finding anything in the mist, so I left the task of tracking the Aluta solely up to my able partner. I did little more than follow him and observe the natural beauty of our new home planet.

John's lack of conversation allowed me to study the geographic wonders that presented themselves with every step. I was observing a strange tree covered in bright purple fruit when a buzzing sound startled me. An Aluta leapt out of the bushes in front of us and even though it was only half his size, it knocked John onto his back and ran past me into a group of shrubs before I could free my pistol. John quickly regained his composure and jumped to his feet with a look of bewilderment.

"What the hell was that all about? By the time I heard the damn thing its knee was in my face!" he said stunned.

"I don't know," I said perplexed, "but it was certainly in a hurry!"

John seemed perturbed that something could surprise him so easily and he quickly shouldered his rifle.

"Well there is only one way to find out," he said adamantly.

Ignoring the path we had been following, we climbed through the thickets from which the Aluta had come. Lacking the thick leathery skin of the Aluta, we took much more time traversing through the thorns and brush of its path than it had and through the pain of torn skin and clothing we learned why they had developed such tough skin. Within moments of following the Aluta's flight path, we heard a series of loud humming and hissing sounds. Just ahead of us was a clearing, and through the brush I could see some movement. We both kneeled near the clearing, and using our hands, pulled the concealing brush aside to get a clear view of the field behind it. The noises we had been hearing were coming from a group of about a dozen Alutas entangled in a large barbed net. The confinement of the net had sent them into a frenzy, and they were fighting, not only with the net, but also with each other. Their teeth tore at both the net and any limb that crossed their path.

Controlling the net was what would become the three hundred and twentieth intelligent alien race known to man. These creatures were about five feet tall and much fuller figured than the Aluta. Every part of their body was fat, including their round pudgy faces. Protruding from the sides of their mouths were two long sharp teeth, one at each corner, that were closer in appearance to tusks than actual teeth. Their skin was a light yellow, and from their clothing, it was obvious they were technically superior to their captives. One of the creatures held the net while the others took turns kicking any Aluta that rolled too close. An Aluta managed to crawl out at the side of one of the nets, but before it could get away, one of its captors knocked it to the ground with a long hammer-like club. Its thin body buckled under the strength of its enemy and fell lifelessly to the ground, oozing blood.

My eyes locked on the vivid scene before me drawing me into a trance. A tap from John awoke me and alerted me to our situation. Several more of these new creatures were beating the brush all around the clearing in hopes of finding more Alutas. One had managed to work his way down toward us and was no more than ten feet away! John was about to raise his rifle when a black form fell from the sky. A heavy black net landed on top of us entangling our heads and limbs. I tried to free myself, but one of the beasts tightened the net, hopelessly trapping me. They dragged us out into the open and began to kick us as we struggled. John's rifle pulled free from his hands when they tightened the net, and although I strained, I couldn't manage to reach the pistol on my hip. They continued to pull the net tighter and tighter until I felt as if I were going to pass out. Suddenly an electric charge shot out from our net and hit one of our captors directly in the face. The charge nearly tore its face apart. In pain it released its grip upon us and fell back holding its head. The net loosened, and in the confusion, I pulled my powder pistol free and fired. I failed to hit anything but the noise from my shot sent our captors running.

Lifting the net off, I looked over at John who still gripped his energy pistol. I could tell from his expression that he wanted to pursue them, but wisely refrained. I had taken several solid blows to my side and fell over when I tried to stand. John rushed over to me and helped me to my feet. His strong exterior body had weathered the blows of our captors much better than mine.

The group of imprisoned Alutas had escaped during the turmoil and the only reminders of our struggle remaining were two empty nets, the body of the Aluta who had been knocked unconscious and the dead body of the beast John had shot. Surprisingly, upon closer examination, I found the Aluta was still breathing. Seeing its poor thin body stretched helplessly out on the ground, I felt a deep compassion for the hardships that it and its people obviously endured. Hunted like wild animals, it appeared they roamed not only to survive but also to stay free.

"Come on," said John, "before they find their balls and hand us ours."

"We can't just leave him here!" I said looking up.

"Sure we can!" he replied. "Besides we'll have a hell of a time lugging it back."

"John, I can't leave him here without making an attempt to save him."

"All right," he said aggravated while pointing toward its body, "under one condition. If at any point it endangers us we leave it. Is that fair?"

"Yes," I said holding the wounded creature.

Reaching behind its thin waist, John picked up its wire-like body as if it were a rag doll and laid it over his left shoulder. I took hold of his energy rifle and we headed back toward our compound.

As we stepped back into the thick brush I couldn't help but hear a comment John made under his breath: "You were easier to get along with when I didn't like you."

# Cosmic Contemplations

# Chapter 6

Traveling as fast as we could on foot, we reached the gate of our little compound late the next evening. We were greeted with both laughter and tears. Cynthia was the first to greet us and I watched, in envy, as she hugged John with compassion that can only be felt between two people who truly love each other. To keep up appearances, Anne came up to give me a hug but I avoided her to greet Edmund and Jenna. I could tell, from her facial expression, that it made her mad, but ever since our conversation in our living quarters, I found myself caring less and less in regards to matters concerning her. After several moments of questions about our trip, the focus of our comrades shifted toward our new companion. He had never regained consciousness and I had feared the entire trip back that he might die at any minute. Cynthia looked him over and after seeing that the creature needed immediate medical attention, rushed it to the infirmary. Dr. Kineard agreed with her decision and called for a meeting to take place as soon as John and I had a chance to clean up.

The meeting following our return was an intense one, but one in which the current dilemma quenched our petty quarrels and united us as a community for the first time. Every vote we took was a unanimous one, which was a first, and every one of us left feeling as if we had accomplished something worthwhile.

First we agreed we would do everything within our power to help the Aluta in our custody to fully recover. We also agreed that it would be in our best interest if he was kept chained up in the barn, for our safety as well as his own and that no one could observe him alone, at least for the time being.

Second we would increase our security and double all guard shifts at night. Cynthia thought it would be best if both John and I went through a full physical in case we had contacted something from our encounter with our newest alien discovery. I hadn't been alone with Cynthia since the incident with her in the pool, but amazingly we didn't experience our usual awkwardness. She examined me as if I was nothing more than a regular patient, and I was glad to know the tension between the two of us had eased.

"Well," she said looking up at me from her clipboard, "everything appears to be fine."

"Good!" I said putting on my shirt.

"I do, however, want you to see me for the next couple days," she said pausing, "just in case."

"Fine… thank you Cynthia," I said while walking over to the door.

I had just stepped out into the hallway when she called me back.

"Oh yeah!" she said excited. "I almost forgot to congratulate you!"

"Do you mind if I ask you on what?"

"You mean Anne hasn't told you yet?" she asked strangely.

"I don't think so," I replied, not having the faintest idea of what she was talking about.

"Oh," she said surprised, "I can't believe she hasn't told you yet. It's been almost three full weeks."

"Since what?" I asked stepping back into her examination room.

"I believe this is something that you should hear from her."

"Listen Cynthia, if there is something unusual about Anne's well being," I said assertively, "then I think I should know immediately, not three weeks later."

"Oh I guess it doesn't really matter, you're going to find out eventually!" she said excited. "You and Anne are going to be our communities' first parents!"

It's hard to explain the overwhelming flow of emotions that swelled up inside of me. Our marriage had been such a charade that Anne and I had never actually consummated it. I turned around and burst out of Cynthia's office nearly breaking the heavy door off its hinges. Anger, frustration, betrayal, jealously, hatred, shock and revenge all struggled to take hold of my conscious.

I walked straight down the hall toward Dr. Kineard's laboratory, ignoring Cynthia's screams to gain my attention. I opened the door and found him alone looking through one of his books. He gave me a furtive glance as I walked in and then continued reading his book, keeping his place with his finger.

"Dr. Adair," he said preoccupied, "I was about to come looking for you, thought we might have a look at your Aluta."

He had barely finished those words when I seized his collar and jerked him around to face me.

"Dr. Adair!" he screamed surprised. "What has come over you?"

"Just when we were starting to pull together as a true community," I said screaming, "you go and mess it all up!"

"Please Dr. Adair," he said tugging on my arms, "I don't know what you are talking about!"

"Anne is pregnant, you son of a bitch!" I yelled choking him.

His whole body went limp after hearing my words, and if it weren't for my grip, he would have collapsed to the floor like a sack of beans.

"You fool!" I yelled shaking him. "This is going to destroy us all! It is going to absolutely tear our community apart!"

His face sunk down into his shoulders and he began to cry.

"We gave up everything to follow you out here beyond anything ever known and this is how you repay us," I said lifting him off the floor. "Say something!"

"I never meant for this to happen!" he said sobbing. "I never meant for this to happen."

"What you've spent nearly a lifetime creating you have managed to destroy with one act!" I declared throwing him onto his lab table, causing a rack of test tubes to fall to the floor and shatter. "This project, our lives, your work," I said pausing, "they're not worth shit now!"

"I'm so sorry!" he cried curling up on his long lab table.

"Well I'm not going to let you destroy my life! No matter how pitiful this little project is, it is all I have!" I said straightening him up and forcing him to look at me. "Everybody else I know outside this fucking project is dead! Do you hear me? Dead!"

"What are we going to do?" he asked looking up at me through the corners of his eyes.

"I am going to tell you exactly what we are going to do! We aren't going to tell a soul about this! Do you understand me?"

"Yes," he answered weakly.

"If anyone finds out then you will lose all credibility and this project will crumble beneath us! We are going to act as if this never happened and you are going to stay away from Anne! That is the only way this is going to work. I'm giving you something that most people don't get... a second chance. Don't mess it up."

I let go of his shirt and left him lying on top of the lab table sobbing. I returned to my room in anger and forced myself to sleep it off.

The next morning I found that Dr. Kineard had decided to spend the day in his quarters to nurse a sudden cold. He refused treatment from Cynthia and never left his room that day. Anne walked around not knowing what to do without her mentor and after dinner retired early to read a book.

I decided to spend my day in the leisure room contemplating our newest predicament. If Dr. Kineard would stay away from Anne, which I was pretty sure he would, Anne and I might actually have the time to form a relationship of substance and raise this child as our own. I began to question if my motives were actually for the benefit of our community or for my own internal aspirations for a relationship with Anne. I hoped that it would satisfy both with the only other course of action being a scandal of immense proportions.

The next day, John and I began working on a few security upgrades for our compound, and John, when it came to military matters, had endless ideas. We used mesh screen to fill the gaps in our energy fence and ran barbed wire along the top of the fence. John had also made dozens of crude but effective four pointed spikes similar to ancient caltrops. We scattered them all around the outside perimeter of our compound to hinder any attempt of an all out assault. We also cut down any vegetation that might allow something to get in or might provide cover for the enemy. Then we sent out numerous motion sensitive remote control camera units that were only around eight inches in length and looked like little boxes on wheels, so that we could observe any enemy movements from the safety of our own compound.

Edmund worked on replanting our external fields, and with Dr. Kineard shunning her, Anne took up with Jenna and helped her translate transmissions from Corvus, our little satellite, of volcanic eruptions that were active on the other side of the planet.

When the work was finished, a wave of pride came over me as I surveyed all the modifications we had completed on our compound, but once I stepped back and examined them more closely, it saddened me. Our compound, which had initially been built to be a part of its natural environment, had now changed to look more like a fortress than a research facility. Tree stumps projected from the ground around our compound for miles in every direction. The untouched beauty that had stunned us at our initial landing was now gone. We had accomplished what our forefathers had been doing since the beginning of time. We had humanized our surroundings.

# Cosmic Contemplations

# Chapter 7

Nearly a week had passed since John and I had encountered and escaped the nets of our newest neighbors on Hipparchus II. Being an alien psychologist, I was given the honor of naming this second species as well. Since I knew nothing about them except their appearance and hunting practices, I gave them the name Chassers. Whether this name was entirely fair or not, only time would tell.

Our wounded Aluta had finally regained consciousness and, during his recovery, I only left his side to eat and sleep. When he first awoke, he immediately tried to run when he saw Edmund and I. Once he discovered he could not, he fell to the floor and conceded our superiority. I spoke to him constantly and just as the encounter with our first Aluta, the movement of my mouth when I spoke astounded him. His motor skills were equivalent to that of intelligent thought and his ability to mimic actions, except those of speech, were excellent. Unfortunately, he was still fearful of us and any attempt to touch him sent him into a panic, making Cynthia's medical treatments nearly impossible. We finally had to resort to tranquilizers to calm him down whenever Cynthia would examine him.

I studied his every emotion and the two he exhibited the most were curiosity and fear. He seemed to be capable of every emotion of human beings, except anger. At no point, even when he felt he was in danger, did he attempt to harm anyone. I know that sometimes there is a thin line between anger and fear, but from my observations I never saw him cross it. Everyone except Jenna and John warmed up to his kind and gentle nature and before long he had earned the nickname

"Hummer". At our last meeting we had placed our compound in a state of emergency and thought it best to have a meeting every week. Since I felt I had learned all I could from him being chained inside a barn, I made a motion at our next meeting that he should be allowed to roam the compound as long as he was secured at all times. Jenna, who was still deathly afraid of him, objected as did John who saw him as only a play toy for a group of over-simulated scientists, but the rest of our group couldn't resist the opportunity to study this new creature out in the open.

Dr. Kineard continued to lead our proceedings, but I could tell he was still uncomfortable around me. When he would motion to me, he would hardly look at me and I noticed, to Anne's frustration, he had been ignoring her in much the same manner. Anne sat in her chair bewildered by her mentor's avoidance and after a few minutes she began to watch me. I wasn't sure if she was catching on to my involvement with Dr. Kineard's sudden change of heart toward her, but by the end of the meeting I felt as uncomfortable around her as Dr. Kineard felt around me. I could feel her eyes peering right through me as I left the room.

After the meeting, I meet up with John, who I figured could help me design a security restraint system for our Aluta while he roamed the compound. He modified one of our remote electrical transmitters that were primarily used to send electrical power from one location to another through the atmosphere. The receiver was attached around the Aluta's waist and whoever held the transmitter could shock him if he tried to run. It was crude and I felt horrible whenever we had to use it, but he was very intelligent and after three unsuccessful attempts to escape he didn't try again. After he realized that he could roam the compound without being shocked, the first place he went was to our outdoor gardens. Much like our previous encounters, he ran into our fields and began to gorge himself, even though we had been feeding him more than he could eat. It appeared to me he didn't seem to understand the concept of ownership and moderation and unfortunately all my endeavors to teach him failed, as all he knew came from a lifetime of scavenging. In the past, to survive, he had to eat whenever he could and to stay free he had run. I stayed with him late that night and through the observation of his sleep patterns came to the conclusion that he experienced stages similar to our own. I had a guard shift with Edmund that night and stayed with Hummer until it came around. Our shift was long and uneventful and once morning came I went to my quarters to catch up on some long needed rest. The excitement of my studies had kept me up around the clock for almost two full Hipparchusian days.

When I got to my quarters, I was surprised to find Anne, especially since I had moved to my own after our last argument. When I walked in, I found her sitting in a chair on the far side of the room. From the expression on her face, I could tell it wasn't going to be a pleasant conversation.

"Long night?"

"Yes," I said, "so can we have this conversation later? I'm really tired."

"Have you noticed how strangely Dr. Kineard has been acting lately?" she asked ignoring my request.

"No, but I'm sure you have," I said in a flat tone while taking off my shirt.

"Well yeah, especially since I haven't seen him for more than two minutes over the past week. You wouldn't happen to know anything about that would you?"

"Listen Anne," I said being short with her, "if you've got something to say, just say it. I'm really not in the mood for this conversation right now."

Her calm inquisitive nature changed as quickly as I said my last sentence and I could see anger surge in her face as she stood up.

"What have you told him to make him be so cold toward me?" she asked raising her voice.

"If you're having problems with the great Dr. Kineard then work them out with him."

"I plan on it."

"Then why are you here bothering me about it?"

"Quit acting so fucking dumb!" she screamed. "I know all about your talk with Charles in the lab last week and I'm warning you to stay out of my personal life!"

"Stay out of your personal life? Anne we are married and I believe that entitles me to some say in the matter."

"When are you going to get this in your thick fucking head? We had an agreement! That's it. There has never been anything between us and there never will be!" she yelled back at me. "Don't you get it? You were nothing more to me than a simple tool to help me get selected for this team. Now I'm done with you and I want you to leave me alone! I have given up entirely too much and eliminated too many obstacles between Charles and I to allow you to screw it all up!"

She stopped and waited for a moment to see if I had a response and, once she realized I didn't, she stormed out of my room leaving me in silence. I had known deep down how she really felt about me long before she so bluntly blurted it out. It was actually hearing it from her mouth that finally destroyed the small glimmer of hope I had secretly harbored for us for so long. My body was exhausted, but my mind continued to churn over our predicament, keeping me awake most of the night. I understood what she meant about giving up so much because every one of us had given up our lives to come here, but what did she mean by eliminating obstacles?

Not being able to keep the whole situation to myself any more, I decided to seek some advice from my friend Edmund. Having the analytical mind of a scientist, I had never taken the time to develop and maintain a true friendship. Everyone who I had considered to be a friend in my life before I became a part of this mission were nothing more than mere acquaintances. The next morning we took a short hike careful to stay within the limits of our observation droids, and found ourselves near the waterfall where I had unsuccessfully tried to take Anne earlier. I told him every detail of my agreement with Anne, as well as my disagreements with both Anne and Dr. Kineard, leaving out only Anne's pregnancy in fear of the negative impact it might cause. As any scientist would, he examined it from every possible aspect and gave me a clear unbiased opinion.

"It sounds to me like you are as much to blame in this as she," he said bluntly. "You made a bad decision and came out here beyond the stars with the intention of turning a relationship with no basis into something meaningful."

"I know Edmund," I said, agreeing with him. "What should I do?"

"I don't think there is anything you can do," he said point blank. "It sounds like she is obsessed with Dr. Kineard and his work and any attempt you or anyone else makes to try and stop it is only going to make matters worse. I'm sorry Alex, I know it's not what you wanted to hear."

"No, but it's what I needed to hear."

"Listen," he said while reaching his arm over my shoulder leading me back toward our compound, "Dr. Kineard is a man of great character and focus and I don't think you have anything to worry about."

"Great character indeed," I replied quietly as we started our walk back toward our protective compound.

On our walk back through the beautiful countryside of Hipparchus II, I decided it would be in the best interest of everyone if I left Anne and Dr. Kineard alone and made the best life I could with the given circumstances. Being alone, I would have plenty of time to devote to my writings that have always been the true passion of my life. I also had lots of new friends and an entire planet to explore. We reached the safety of our gates just before nightfall and were greeted by John and Cynthia who had already geared up to come and look for us.

"Who needs kids with you two wandering off all the time!" grumbled John in his own good humor. "I've had dogs with less maintenance than you two!"

"Sorry," I answered, "we didn't realize how late it had gotten."

Within moments, everyone except our new recluse Dr. Kineard came out to greet us. Anne seemed to be in an unusually pleasant mood and completely stunned me with a gentle kiss and hug. Not knowing how to respond to her, I stood still failing to return her kind greeting. She tugged on my hand to follow her as if we were schoolyard sweethearts and when I refused she whispered in my ear.

"Come on silly," she said. "I want to talk to you about something."

I waved goodbye to everyone and followed her to her quarters like a helpless schoolboy. Once we got in she told me to take a seat at the table and went into the next room. Within a few minutes she returned in a long white dress carrying two plates of food. She placed one in front of me and sat down softly across from me staring into my eyes.

"I hope you like it," she said twirling her long hair.

"What is this all about Anne?" I asked mistrusting. "Yesterday you told me to stay out of your life and now you're fixing me dinner?"

"I know, I was just angry about the way Dr. Kineard had been treating me and I'm sorry I took it out on you. Do you forgive me?" she asked in a cute humble way.

Anne had always been a person of strong character and her sudden submissive behavior took me off guard.

"Is that the only reason you asked me here?" I asked skeptically.

"No," she answered, "I also asked you here to talk about us."

"What about you and Dr. Kineard?" I asked sampling a bit of food.

"That's over," she replied casually stirring her food with her fork.

"What happened?"

"I spoke with him after we argued in your room yesterday and I realized that my love for him had been nothing but an admiration for his work," she said pausing for a moment before continuing, "a type of puppy love."

"And now all that is over, just like that?"

"Yes," she said coolly, "what would I have to gain from making all this up? I want the two of us to start over and give this marriage a fair chance. See where it might lead."

"I'm sorry if I sound a little apprehensive, but you've jumped from one side of the spectrum to the other in regards to your attitude toward me in less than a day."

"I don't blame you after how I have treated you," she said supportively. "I just hope you don't let your distrust of me keep us apart."

We finished dinner, saying very little, and once we were done she got up and slowly walked behind me.

"Come on," she whispered into my ear as she slowly massaged my shoulders, "there's something else I want to show you."

I turned around and watched her walk over to the bed. She sat down slowly and began to gently rub her hand across the sheets.

"Come here," she said laughing a little, "It's not like we're not married."

Her smooth cream-colored dress was long at the bottom and cut low at the top letting her hair lay softly against her bare skin. Her skin, a soft white tone, almost matched the color of her dress perfectly and if it wasn't for the frills on her dress I wouldn't have been able to see where one ended and the other began. She was beautiful and she knew it. I got up and sat down next to her wondering if she really meant what she said about the two of us or if she was just spinning a web of deceit. In a moment of passion, I discarded all my suspicions and took a chance.

# Cosmic Contemplations

# Chapter 8

Early the next morning, a series of knocks awoke me from my sleep. Even though Anne was still lying next to me, I could hardly believe what had happened between us. I got up and cracked the door to see who was seemingly beating it off its hinges. It was Edmund.

"Alex!" he said frantically. "Hummer got away last night!"

"What?" I said. "I'll be right out!"

I began to rummage around the room and gather my clothes. Anne rose up not bothering to cover herself.

"What's wrong?"

"They found Hummer missing this morning," I answered while putting on my socks.

"What are you going to do?"

"I'm not sure about everybody else, but I'm going to see if I can find him before it's too late."

"Here, let me fix you something to take with you."

"I don't have time, but thanks anyway," I said grabbing my backpack and heading for the door.

"Here at least take this," she said handing me a small package of rolls.

I put them into my pack and gave her a kiss.

I stepped out into the morning light to find myself the last one, besides Anne, to make it outside. Edmund came up to me and bumped my shoulder.

"We can't find Anne anywhere. You wouldn't happen to know where she might be would you?" he said winking as if he had a handful of dust in his eye.

I ignored his question in hopes that he would quit teasing me about Anne and asked how Hummer had escaped. According to Dr. Kineard, he had apparently chewed through his binding and escaped under the cover of night. Everyone thought it would be best if we let him go, but John finally volunteered to accompany me when he realized that nothing was going to keep me from going after him. He went back inside and returned in a few minutes carrying two energy rifles, an energy pistol and my closed powder pistol.

He handed me a rifle and as he handed me my old pistol he said, "Here you go, cowboy."

I thanked him and buckled it on my hip. Edmund volunteered to go with us, but I refused to let him in fear of completely depleting our compound's defense. We hastily left the camp in hopes of finding Hummer before he got too far from our base. As far as we knew, he was still wearing our receiver around his waist and was probably still within the range of our transmitter, but not knowing what kind of trouble he might be in, we decided not to use it unless we had visual contact with him.

John took up his trail within seconds of leaving our compound and we began our search without delay. I could tell from John's expressions that he couldn't understand my desire to catch a creature that obviously didn't want to be kept in captivity. What he didn't understand was that a creature that had experienced nothing but a lifetime of fear and pain, even from his own people, couldn't grasp that we meant to help him. He was a tortured soul with a good heart and I wanted to give him a chance to experience something besides the mere desire to survive.

We were only a day and a half travel from the meadow were we had first encountered the Chassers and if we couldn't catch up with Hummer before then, we decided that it would be best to turn back. We traveled the entire day without stopping and when night fell we turned to our night vision goggles without stopping. I ate several of Anne's biscuits with beaming pride, and even though they tasted bland, I was sure they would help me keep up my strength. It amazed me how someone so beautiful could cook something that tasted so bad. We finally stopped to rest our eyes as they began to tire under the strain of the lime green light emitted by our goggles. John had brought a two man pressure bubble and inflated it so we could at least be protected from the elements while we slept. I feel asleep as soon as I rolled in and didn't move a muscle until John woke me the next morning.

For some reason, I felt groggy as I rose to my feet, but I blamed it on the prior day's long hike. As the day wore on, I found it more difficult to keep up with the long strides of John. I could tell he was pulling up for me but he wouldn't admit it. I cursed my lack of conditioning and finally had to stop and rest from near muscle collapse. John sat down beside me, unconcerned if we found Hummer or not, and consoled me by saying that we probably wouldn't ever find such a little guy on such a big planet anyway. Determined to find Hummer, I ignored the pain that seemed to suddenly ravage my abdominal area and forced myself to carry on. I was struggling to my feet, when John's big hand grasped my jacket and jerked me back down. He made a motion with his other hand for me to be quiet and then pointed through the bushes ahead of us.

Barely twenty feet ahead was a group of Chassers using long sticks to prod and beat the brush. We both freed our rifles from our back holsters and took prone firing positions. There were only six of them and from the best I could tell none of them had projectile weapons. John switched his energy current bar from stun to kill and took aim. They were progressively working in our direction and it would be just a matter of moments before we were subjected to their search. It appeared they were performing some type of policing action, as if they had already seen, heard or captured some previous game. I could only hope that we weren't too late for Hummer. After a few moments they stopped to discuss something and I thought we might have caught a break, but to our dismay, they split up and three of them continued to work their way toward us. I could tell John was getting antsy and I wasn't sure if he would be able to hold off his trigger or not. I reached back and pulled my pistol free from its holster and brought it up in case all hell broke loose. Within moments they were less than ten feet away from us and with each step they made the tenser our situation became. I could feel each drop of sweat that rolled down my head and hear every beat of my heart.

We were no farther than two feet from the edge of the tree line and once they were in front of us, we would be close enough to reach out and touch them. The beating began to get so loud that I could have almost screamed at the top of my lungs and not been heard. One of them stood directly in front of me and began to beat the branches and brush all around me. His pole struck me twice and I was sure he was going to notice me. After the third time his pole struck me, he stopped swinging his pole and began to move the foliage around with his hand. A fat round face protruded through the bushes in front of me. I pointed my pistol at it and was about to fire directly into its face, when a crash in the bushes to the left of us caused me to hold back on the trigger. Hummer had been hiding in the brush barely twenty feet away! He broke through the brush, running from his pursuers. All the Chassers, including the one who was standing only a few inches away from me, took to chase. John and I breathed a long sigh of relief.

"Come on," said John whispering to me through the brush, "let's get out of here while the getting is good."

"We can't leave him," I claimed, "he just saved us!"

"It was because of him that we got into this mess and he only ran to save his own hide!" he yelled under his breath.

"I won't leave him in the hands of those beasts!" I declared.

"Alright," said John unenthusiastically raising his rifle, "let's go and get the little shit!"

Unlike Hummer, the Chassers appeared to be no faster than us, which made the pursuit effortless through the sparse forest of Hipparchus II. As the hunt continued, many of the creatures began to grunt and chant wildly in strange unison. I wasn't sure if their screams were from pure excitement or if they were meant in some way to keep their prey on the move, but either way, the noise made it easy for us to follow them without being heard. I stayed directly behind John and we followed them until we felt Hummer had gotten away.

We were about to slip off into a large tree line when our fortunes changed for the worse. One of the Chassers happened to turn around before we made the thick brush along the clearing's tree line. The three of us become aware of each other at precisely the same time. It made an attempt to scream, but John fired his energy rifle and caught it directly in the mouth, frying its vocal chords and silencing it forever. Its burnt body fell lifelessly to the ground releasing its soul in a puff of black smoke. The loud burst of energy emitted from John's rifle made a loud thunderclap as it struck its target, alerting the rest of the Chassers. Upon seeing us, the whole group scattered. I fired my pistol twice, missing both times, while John managed to kill one and wound another before they could take cover in the forest. As I fired into the forest two more times in hopes of scaring them away, something whizzed past my head. John fell to the ground immediately and returned fire.

"Get down!" he screamed. "They are shooting at us!"

I fell down beside him and fired two more blind shots into the forest. We heard two more whizzings come from within the forest as something struck the ground just in front of us and bounced over our heads.

"How the hell are they shooting at us?" I asked in bewilderment.

"Get up and run to that tree behind us," commanded John, "I'll cover you."

I waited a second to catch my breath, jumped to my feet and sprinted. We had been caught in what was almost a completely round clearing with only a few trees in the center. Things began to zip all around me as I ran, hitting the ground and trees in front of me. Amazingly, I made the cover of the trees without incident and fell down behind their roots. Shards of metal struck the trunk I was lying behind splintering small wood fragments down upon me. Listening, I could hear John's rifle firing in retaliation, still laying cover fire. Not stopping to catch my breath, I pulled my energy rifle free from my back holster and began to fire long bolts into the edge of the forest.

John took my cue and made his own run toward the cover of my defensive position. One of my shots hit the trunk of a dead tree and caused it to erupt into flames. Fortunately, John made it to the safety of the trees in the middle of the clearing without being hit, digging in next to me.

"Now what?" I asked him.

"I don't know," he replied honesty. "They seem to have a strong military organization and if my guess is correct, I bet one went back to get help, while these keep us pinned down. The longer we wait the worse our situation is going to become."

"Which way should we run?" I asked him.

"That is just what they want us to do," he said leaning around the tree and firing. "They are without doubt hunters by trade and if we run, we are only going to play into their hands. The best way to stop a hunter is to take the hunt to them."

"Are you crazy?" I asked him dumbfounded.

"Would you rather be chasing them or have them chase you?" he asked quickly.

"I can't believe I'm saying this, but lead the way."

"Well, you are a reasonable man after all," he said, smiling. "Okay, see if you can't catch a few more of those trees on fire and when I signal you, I want you to run straight into those woods. Once we get inside, their projectiles won't be as effective and we can use the technology of our weapons to muscle them around."

Both of us quit firing into the darkness of the forest and began to fire at the more vulnerable treetops. We kept our charges long and constant until the particular tree we were firing at caught fire. Smoke began to billow all around the forest in front of us and flames began to dance onto the ground below. After a few moments the fire we had been taking from the woods ceased.

"All right cowboy, let's raise a few acres of hell," he said rising to his feet.

We both jumped to our feet and ran across the clearing, making the forest's edge without any resistance. John holstered his rifle and pulled his energy pistol free for possible close quarter combat. Following John's example, I did the same and took hold of my powder pistol. John's keen hunting eyes picked up the movement of one of our foes and he took chase. Little pieces of ash and fire began to fall around us and before I could follow his lead, I began to lose my breath. My diaphragm tightened and every breath I took became a struggle with death. I wasn't sure if I had inhaled too much smoke but suddenly I lost my balance and fell to the ground. Everything began to swirl around and within seconds my vision went completely black. The last thing I remember was the sound of crackling fire and John's pistol firing off into the distance.

When I awoke, I found myself strapped down to a medical bed in one of Dr. Cynthia Berman's examining rooms.

"We thought we were going to lose you," she said while gently caressing my head. Her soft hands stroked my forehead in a kind and caring manner, a type of love I had not felt since my mother had coddled me as a child.

"What happened?" I asked while trying to free myself from the straps that were holding me down securely.

"Relax," she said softly, "I will explain everything to you in a moment. Right now I need you to lie still and let me finish what I have started."

It is during difficult times that a man discovers who his real loved ones truly are. Edmund spent every waking moment with me, save for when he had guard duty. He spent so much time with me that Anne began to complain about never being able to see me alone. Staying with her new change of heart, Anne came and saw me everyday, as did Cynthia, although her visits were primarily for medical reasons. Even John, who would like everyone to believe he didn't have feelings, came and saw me a couple of times. The only person who failed to come and see me was Dr. Kineard, who everyone claimed was rarely seen anymore.

I began to get stronger each day, under the guidance of the very knowledgeable Dr. Berman, and before long I was able to stand and walk around a little. I found out that somehow I had contracted renale poisoning. The strange thing was that renale had only been found on one planet and that planet was nearly forty thousand light years away. Being a poison that originated from the flower of a harkarl plant, Edmund knew quite a bit about it and had been the one who had brought my symptoms to Dr. Berman's attention. If it had not been for him, I would have surely died. As I had mentioned earlier, Edmund had been by my side since the beginning and it was he that tried to come up with a hypothesis on how I could have come in contact with such a strange and distant poison. His only conclusion was that there must have been a plant almost identical in nature to the harkarl and that it must have caught fire exposing me to its harmful fumes. It seemed like a stretch of the imagination even to him, but it had to be the only possible explanation.

# Cosmic Contemplations

# Chapter 9

Thanks to Cynthia's excellent medical attention and the watchful eyes of both Anne and Edmund, I was back on my feet by the end of the week. I found out, through Edmund, that John had carried me home after he had found me unconscious. As for what had happened to the Chassers, I didn't ask for fear of learning about their certain demise. Knowing John, he did what was best for our survival. That was how he analyzed everything. If it was in the name of survival, it was what had to be done. Sometimes, I wished that I could act in that very same manner. Upon his return, he went into a fervor updating our defenses based on what he had learned from our last encounter with the Chassers.

His first defense was to build bunkers to protect us from their strange missile fire. He had managed to bring one of their missile weapons back with him. It wrapped around the arm almost like a primitive bracer and fired small metal like bullets, which could be easily loaded into its top. It was based on a simple but highly effective compression spring that could be cocked by a lever. It was a crude invention, but one typical of a developing species much like we were eight thousand years ago. In the field of alien psychology, I had seen it a hundred times. Every species I had ever studied that exhibited any form of developing intelligence always placed the development of weapons as their highest priority. That was why I had been so interested in Hummer and his unique species. They certainly held a level of intellect above that of most life forms, but they didn't seem to show any aptitude for violence. They were the only species I had seen that lived in complete harmony with their surroundings. It was as if on this tiny little moon we were witnessing a war between the best and worst traits of man. The Chassers represented our inclination toward brutality while the Alutas our humanity. It appeared that once again hatred would defeat kindness as it always had throughout recorded history. Unfortunately, with the actions of our last encounter, we had chosen sides, a decision that would return to haunt us.

Without the mentorship of Dr. Kineard, Anne moved her research to a different lab and consequently we spent more time together. Her attitude toward me had shifted so quickly that it almost seemed like a dream. I spent my days between her, Edmund and my writings, leaving me little time for anything else. I returned to swimming twice a day and every so often Cynthia would join me. My renewed relationships with Anne and John had wiped away the tension between Cynthia and I and we were finally able to be alone without feeling awkward. It was as if we were all living in the Garden of Eden, with no shameful past, a fresh beginning and a limitless future. I never had or dreamed of such happiness, but just as the Garden of Eden had its catastrophic ending, the past would repeat itself and so would ours. It all began with a visit from my best friend Edmund. I was in my quarters about to start writing when he knocked on the door.

"Come on in," I said while looking through my computer files.

"Hey Alex."

"Oh, hello Edmund," I said politely. "Come on in and make yourself comfortable."

"Is Anne around?"

"She just left," I said noticing his strange behavior.

"Do you know when she will be back?"

"Oh no!" I said looking over to him laughing. "You two aren't having some type of disagreement are you?"

"Alex," he said apprehensively while rubbing his hands together, "there is something I have been wanting to talk to you about."

I could tell from his voice that something was really bothering him, so I dropped my comedy, leaned forward and motioned for him to continue.

"You know we never really figured out how you contacted renale poisoning."

"I thought we had determined that I must have been exposed to something similar to it during the forest fire John and I started."

"Well, that was the only explanation I could possibly conceive at the time, but I believe that there may be another possibility," he said grimly.

"What, that someone poisoned me?" I asked joking again.

"Alex," he said seriously, "I checked the main computer files and a small amount of renale extract was brought along with some of Dr. Kineard's chemicals, but when I spoke to Dr. Kineard about it, he couldn't verify its whereabouts."

"What are you saying Edmund, that somebody in the compound poisoned me?" I asked again, but this time my face was gripped with concern.

"I don't know, but there is something else," he said with a long pause. "I don't think that the death of Dr. Kineard's wife was an accident."

I actually believe at that moment my heart stopped beating. It was if our Garden of Eden had changed into the pit of hell in the short amount of time it took him to say one sentence. Completely immersed in shock, I couldn't respond and continued to listen, while my stomach churned uncomfortably.

"I took the time to examine the computer's mainframe, but all records concerning the cryogenic chambers have been erased," he said.

"Do you think it was Anne?" I asked nervously not really wanting to hear his answer.

"I can't say with absolute certainty, but if we could get into the cryogenic's records we could find out whose chamber, if any, opened early."

"I guess we have no choice but to return to the ship and pull those files," I said lethargically.

"Wait," said Edmund, "if someone did do this, they are obviously not above stooping to murder. If someone really did kill Jane and tried to poison you, they might take even more drastic measures to stop us."

"What should we do then?" I asked half-hearted.

"We can check it out tomorrow morning. We'll tell everybody that we are going out to gather a few samples for my work. Then, by this time tomorrow we'll know the truth," he said with a stern look and continued, "whatever it might be."

Edmund could see how painful the subject was for me, so he decided to leave me alone and get ready for our trip tomorrow. The conversation drained every ounce of my strength and made me sick to my stomach. Lying down on my bed, I wondered what we would discover in those files and if I wanted to find out at all. If the situation was based only on my poisoning, I would actually look the other way for Anne and me to have a chance but another life might have been taken and if so, justice had to be served no matter how many lives would be affected. I loved her so much and couldn't bear to see her with mixed feelings, so I spent the day in our library. We had designed a small reading corner that couldn't be seen when a person entered the room and I hid there, among my work, for the entire day.

Anne came looking for me twice but I ignored her calls and stayed in the corner. My mind kept drifting back to the situation at hand and I failed to accomplish any writing. It was true that Dr. Kineard was the only one who had access to his chemicals, but since Anne had been intimate with him, she would have certainly been able to get to the renale extract. I traded guard shifts with John, to stay away from Anne, and left with Edmund early that morning, never saying a word to her.

We left at the crack of the first sunrise and were well beyond the sight of our compound before the rising of the second. Our ship was barely an hour hike from our compound and we reached it before either of us broke a sweat. We found it in good shape and, after breaking its seal, found ourselves inside its vast interior within minutes. It seemed a lifetime had passed since I had seen it last. Not wasting any time, Edmund turned on the ship's main computer and restored its power. I checked the seal on the cryogenic chamber of the late Jane Kineard and discovered that the seal had a long slit in it. I'm not an expert on seal tearing, but the seal itself didn't appear to exhibit any signs of wear or deterioration.

"Alex!" yelled Edmund. "The computer is just about up."

I walked over to him and waited to see what we would find.

"Computer, user 12c requests access," said Edmund into the thin air.

*"User 12c voice verification verified. Access approved,"* answered a monotone voice.

"Computer," he said again, "open the cryogenic history file."

*"All cryogenic history files have been cleansed,"* recited the computer.

"Computer, who authorized their cleansing?" asked Edmund.

*"Information requested is not currently available,"* stated the computer.

"Computer, restore all cryogenic history files," ordered Edmund.

*"Restoration of all cryogenic history files initiated,"* stated the computer.

"Hopefully we can restore enough information to piece together what might have happened," Edmund said to me.

"Yeah," I said half-heartedly.

*"Restoration of requested files is complete,"* said the computer.

"Computer, who authorized the cleansing of these files?" asked Edmund again.

*"Information requested is not currently available,"* stated the computer.

"Computer, state the number of openings of cryogenic chambers one through eight since launch," said Edmund.

*"Chamber one, one opening... chamber two, one opening... chamber three, one opening... chamber four, one opening... chamber five, one opening... chamber six, one opening... chamber seven, two openings... chamber eight, one opening,"* stated the computer.

As I heard that chamber seven had two openings my head sunk down onto my chest. Anne must have set her chamber to open early and cut a slit in Jane's before programming her own to open a second time with the rest of the group. She knew that Jane's chamber would lose pressure and not stop her from aging, leaving Dr. Kineard unattached and free from the obligations of his marriage. I could only assume that she would have done the same to me if she had known the trouble I was going to cause her later. I realized that my strange and almost deadly exposure to renale poisoning probably wasn't an accident either. Being a man of reason, Edmund wasn't sure how to console me, but he tried all the same.

"I'm sorry Alex," he said, touching my shoulder.

"No hard feelings," I said, "but I really don't want to talk about it."

He stepped aside and left me alone. I leaned back against the wall and slid down to my knees. It was the first time I had wept since I was a child. After a few moments, which seemed like hours, I rose to my feet and tried to hide any signs that I had cried. Edmund came back into the room and we decided that we should return as soon as possible.

"Computer, print a hard copy of your last report," said Edmund.

"*Access is denied,*" stated the computer.

"Computer, user 12c requests access," said Edmund quickly.

"*User 12c access has been overridden,*" stated the computer.

"Computer, who has superseded my access?" asked Edmund.

"*Requested information is denied,*" stated the computer.

Edmund turned to me with a baffled look and shrugged his shoulders.

"Computer, user 33x requests access," I said.

"*User 33x access is denied,*" stated the lifeless voice.

I was about to try again when a loud rally of clicks and buzzers sounded interrupting me. Before we knew what was happening, the lights went off and I heard the ship's main door close and lock.

"Computer, what functions did you just perform?" asked Edmund.

"*Lockup and shutdown has been authorized,*" it stated.

Edmund turned on his flashlight and began to look around.

"Computer, reverse your last set of actions," ordered Edmund.

"*Access is denied,*" it reported.

Edmund shined his light on me and asked, "What does this mean?"

"Computer, exactly what do the functions lockup and shutdown consist?" I asked standing in the dark.

"*All systems have been shut off, all exits have been locked and the ship is now pressurized,*" it reported carelessly.

"Computer, we did not authorize this command. Who authorized this command?" I asked.

"*The authorization code was received through an outside transmission. Access to user I.D. is denied,*" it reported.

"Computer, input authorization code delta, lima, foxtrot six," I said.

"*Delta, lima, foxtrot six is invalid,*" it stated.

"Edmund someone has changed the computer's main authorization code!" I said in terror.

Edmund ran over to the main hatch and tried to release it with the emergency lever.

"Alex," yelled Edmund in fear, "the hatches will not open!"

"Check all the other exits while I try to gain access to the computer manually," I yelled back to him from across the room.

I could see his small light bouncing up and down as he left for the rear of the ship. I pulled out a flashlight of my own and opened a panel below the computer's main screen. A small keyboard protruded out slowly and finally stopped in front of my fingertips. I began to type, but my keystrokes produced nothing and then suddenly the computer interrupted me.

"*Keyboard access is denied.*"

I continued to type.

"*Keyboard access is denied,*" it stated again.

I leaned back in my chair and kicked the keyboard in frustration. In a few minutes Edmund came back with a look of dread in his eyes.

"All the exits have been sealed and I'm afraid that the ship has sealed us off from the outside atmosphere completely!"

"Computer, what is our current internal oxygen level?" I asked nervously.

"*Current level is at 99.6%,*" it reported.

"Computer, Open all external vents," I ordered.

"*Access is denied.*"

"Computer, turn on the internal oxygen supply," I said loudly.

"*Access is denied,*" it stated again.

"Damn!" I yelled in anger. "That fucking murdering bitch has trapped us in here!"

"Alex," yelled Edmund, "calm down. Let's try and be productive here. Certainly two intelligent men can figure a way to get out of here!"

"How much time do you think we have?" I asked him trying to calm down.

"I don't know for sure," he said looking around. "Maybe twenty four hours if we're lucky, but one thing for sure is that we're not going to get anywhere with this computer. Anne has changed all the authorization codes and invalidated our status. She is holding all the cards. I believe we both grossly underestimated her."

Edmund was right. She was running the show. Our little trip out here, to expose her, played right into her hands. Nobody would find us in time, especially since we had given false information on our whereabouts. I had no doubt that John would come looking for us when we didn't return, but he'd start in the wrong direction, toward Edmund's sample fields. They would eventually find us, but only in time for a burial. I was sure if Anne had set us up, she also had a plan to make our deaths appear a horrible accident, much as she had Dr. Kineard's wife. Edmund, a botanist, and I a writer knew less about the ship than any other members of our crew. There is nothing worse than being a man of intelligence and reason and being out of your field of expertise. We had the intelligence to take any actions needed, but just didn't have access to the required information.

"First let's try and figure out how to stop our loss of oxygen," I said trying to reason through the situation the best I could. "We have to either let it in from the outside or get it out of the ship's internal storage."

Edmund pulled a knife from his hip holster and said, "I'll go and see if there are any seals that I might be able to compromise."

"Good," I said responding, "and I'll go and see if there is any kind of manual valve to the ship's oxygen tanks."

Edmund's light marched off toward the rear of the ship while I went below to the main cargo hold. We might die but it wouldn't be from a lack of effort on our part. After several minutes, I found the ship's three large oxygen tanks in good condition, but without any type of external valve. I pulled my pistol free and contemplated shooting a hole in one, but refrained in fear of blowing us to pieces. After a few more minutes, with no success, I climbed back up to the main deck and found Edmund with the same look of exasperation.

"All the seals are internally compressed in the door chambers," he said sadly. "I couldn't even get close to puncturing them. We will have to find another way."

I nodded and sat down for a moment.

"The tanks are hopeless too," I said. "It looks as if we are going to have to go back to the old drawing board."

"Computer," I yelled from my dark corner, "what is our current internal oxygen level?"

"*Current level is at 99.2%,*" it reported calmly.

"Stop breathing so much," I said to Edmund.

"I assure you," he said seriously, "I am not breathing more than my fair share."

"I know," I said, "I was joking, just trying to lighten things up a bit."

"Well I may not be much of a comedian, but I do believe that that was in bad taste."

"Wait," I yelled jumping up to my feet pointing to Edmund. "That's it!"

My sudden outburst startled him and he nearly fell over.

"If we can't get anymore oxygen in here, we'll have to stop using it!" I said proudly.

"I don't quite understand your proposal," he said curiously.

"The cryogenic chambers my good friend," I said pointing at him as if I had just made a breakthrough discovery, "we'll use the cryogenic chambers! They are set to manually override the computer in case of failure. The computer uses its internal oxygen tanks to support them."

"But they will put us under and if Anne is still monitoring the main computer she will know they are in use and I don't want to be unconscious with that woman on the loose."

"That's why only one of us will get in!" I said triumphantly. "The other person can stay and guard until John finds us!"

"He will never suspect us to be in here."

"Don't you worry about that Edmund I have a plan to get somebody down here real quick!" I said smiling.

# Cosmic Contemplations

# Chapter 10

Edmund crawled into his cryogenic chamber and set it for a forty eight hour cycle. He looked at me nervously as cool gases encircled his body and rushed into his lungs peacefully dragging him into unconsciousness. As soon as he was asleep, I reprogrammed his chamber opening for two months instead of two days in case we were not discovered in time. Then, I closed a second chamber and set its timer for the same time as Edmund's. If Anne was monitoring the ship's computer, I knew she would come after us to finish the job she started and if not, then maybe John would find us in time. I estimated that my oxygen supply would last about two days if I was fortunate or at least a day and a half. I sat perfectly quiet for fear of Anne monitoring the computer. For my plan to work, she had to believe that the two of us were trying to wait her out by hibernating in our cryogenic chambers.

I chose a dark corner to the left and rear of the main hatch for my vigil and waited in the dark silence of what might become my tomb. As the hours passed, my legs started to cramp and my eyes began to slump closed. I wasn't sure if it was from lack of oxygen or just from sitting still in the dark for so long, but for fear of Anne, I couldn't check my oxygen level with the computer. I was sure that after tonight when we didn't return, John would come out looking for us and therefore make the situation more desperate for Anne. I could only hope that my plan was clever enough to outsmart my beautiful and cunning wife.

The sound of the main hatch opening awoke me from my sleep and I quickly pulled my pistol from its holster. The bright light from outside caught my eyes directly, shrinking my pupils, temporarily blinding me. Not able to see, I closed my eyes and sat, without flinching, hoping that whoever it was would not notice me before my sight returned. When my eyesight finally restored, the image of my murderous wife stood in the shadows creeping toward the ship's cryogenic chamber room. She moved like a cat through the darkness ready to pounce on her prey.

I pulled up my pistol, took aim and cocked the lever.

"Hello dear," I said rising to my feet.

She spun around with amazing quickness.

"I'm so glad you found us sweetie," I said in a loving tone. "It seems the computer went haywire and tried to kill us. You wouldn't happen to know anything about that would you?"

Her facial expression instantly changed from one of fear to kindness as quickly as someone turning on a light switch.

"Alex," she said walking toward me slowly, "I have changed. That is why I came down here… to tell you that I have fallen in love with you."

"Stop right where you are," I said pointing my gun at her. "You try and turn this ship into our coffin and when that fails, I catch you sneaking in here to finish us off and you claim you have changed?"

"I have really!" she cried. "The reason all this stuffed failed is that the ship's main computer crashed erasing all its files and reset the codes. I only wanted a chance to explain everything to you before you did something drastic! Please Alex! You have to believe me! Don't give up on us!"

"Why didn't you tell everybody else we were here? They have to be out looking for us by now," I said angrily.

"Because I wanted a chance to explain myself to you before you told the whole group about what I did to Jane!" She fell down to her knees and began to sob into her hands. "God, don't you think I would take it all back if I could? I would do anything to bring her back so we could be together! I would give up my own life if it would help, but it won't… It won't!"

I had never seen her cry real tears. I wanted to reach over and hold her in my arms… if only I could believe her.

"Why did you make me love you after it was too late for us?" she screamed. "Why?"

# Intergalactic Eden

As I watched her weeping on the floor, I wasn't sure exactly how I was going to handle the situation. Edmund knew too much to cover it up and since I couldn't bring myself to kill an unarmed and pregnant woman, my only choice was to bring her and the predicament out into the open. I held my hand down to her and helped her up from the floor. Tears ran down her grief stricken face and as I peered into them, I wished we were back on the launching pad so that the two of us might start anew. Knowing what I knew now, I might have been able to save her and maybe even us. Suddenly she swung her arm from behind her back crashing a short metal bar against the side of my face, knocking me to the floor. Warm salty blood poured into my right eye, as I lay on the ground nearing unconsciousness. I rose up groggily, but still with a clean shot as she jumped out the main hatch. I held the gun unable to pull the trigger. I had a deep laceration about two inches long on my forehead seeping blood over my face. I pulled off my shirt and used it to clot the wound before freeing Edmund. It took him several minutes to recuperate from his cryogenic sickness, but once he could actually focus his eyes my face was his only concern. We made the trip back and were both glad to see that Anne had not returned. Cynthia rushed to my aid and once she was finished closing up my cut, we held an emergency meeting.

What I did at the meeting was the hardest thing I had ever done in my entire life. I stood up in front of our committee and explained the whole situation in detail, from beginning to end, leaving out only the details of Anne's pregnancy. I thought I could at least save Dr. Kineard the embarrassment of everyone knowing that he had bedded with the woman who had murdered his wife, as he was as much a victim of Anne's treachery as any of us. When the part about his wife's murder was revealed, his face turned white as powdered sugar and his limp body collapsed to the floor. Cynthia rushed over to help him and before long had him back onto his feet.

I was so ashamed of my involvement in Anne's plan and our sham marriage that I couldn't bear to look into the faces of my community. When I finished, the room was so silent that the sound of a pin dropping would have burst an eardrum. Even John, who had an opinion about everything, was speechless. After several long awkward moments, everyone left without speaking, leaving me alone in shame. If only I hadn't been stupid enough to accept Anne's proposal, they would have had a real chance for a new beginning instead of this horrible catastrophe that would haunt us forever. After I was sure everyone had left, I returned to my quarters and locked the door. I threw away everything that I could find of hers in hopes of forgetting her, but it was no use. I could see her in my mind as clearly as if she was standing in front of me. Take it from a physiatrist there is nothing worse than to hate someone you love. It tears you apart both physically and mentally.

The next morning, as if things weren't bad enough, I awoke to the sounds of sirens. I jumped out of bed and frantically dressed in the dim red light from my room's emergency siren. I meet Edmund and Jenna in the hall and could tell from their expressions they were just as bewildered by the alarm as I. The three of us ran down the hall toward the exit of the east wing. The only thing I could think of at that moment was what dwelled upon my mind, Anne. Maybe somebody had spotted her and pulled the alarm, which put us in another predicament. What would we do if we caught her? I don't believe any of us could put her to death or even banish her, yet alone build her a prison to live in the rest of her days. And what of the child she nourished in her womb? I had hoped she would disappear from our lives forever, if not in thought, at least in presence. I know it's cruel to wish that upon a woman and innocent child, but at that moment it was what I wanted. When we reached the interns of our compound, what we found was worse than a captured Anne... far worse.

The Chassers had found our compound and were about to make war on us in a style that could only be described as medieval. I told Edmund and Jenna to bring back every weapon they could carry from the armory and ran over to the gate to see how bad our situation had become. There were hundreds marching slowly toward our compound, pushing giant siege weapons of war. Bright flags flapped in the wind and smoke rose up all around their formations. Between each column of soldiers were rows of Chassers carrying long poles, twice the height of an average man, hoisted into the air. Thick black smoke brewed from the fire at their end and within a few moments the whole formation of soldiers was cloaked with swirling smoke. Edmund and Jenna returned with arms full of energy rifles and pistols. Cynthia took up a post with John, while Edmund, Jenna and I took positions in a separate ground bunker.

"Where is Dr. Kineard?" I asked Edmund.

"He is near a nervous breakdown. Cynthia as well as the rest of us didn't think he would be of much use in such a situation."

It bothered me that they had all met and discussed things in private, but considering the circumstances, I understood. I was, at the moment what they referred to in close-knit groups, as out of the loop.

"Don't worry my good friend," he said seeing my disappointment. "No one blames you for what has happened. We just need a little time to cope with it all."

I gave him a kind glance for his words and refocused on our current predicament. We watched their slow progress by the high tops of their siege weapons and began to fire into the thick smoke once it came into range. Occasionally, I could hear what sounded like a scream or cry of agony as bolts from our weapons disappeared into the obscurity, but the large black cloud continued to move without showing any signs of halting. Now I knew what the men of Earth felt during an ancient siege. As the dark cloud of smoke got closer, John began to yell orders down to us.

"Alex," he said screaming, "move over to the southeast bunker to keep them from getting in there, but whatever you do, don't shoot directly into the fence it might short it out leaving us defenseless!"

I nodded to him and did as I was told. I had seen him react in military matters first hand and knew this was his forte. I scrambled to my new post, being careful to stay below our screened in fence line. Only a few moments passed before we were in the range of their primitive bullets and sparks began to shoot off our fence as they struck it in a flurry of blows. We continued to fire our rifles as best we could, but their cover fire held us in check below the walls of our bunkers. John got off a good shot and caught the top of one of their rolling siege towers on fire. It began to crackle and burn, but its unseen crew continued to roll it ever so slowly toward us.

Following John's example, I quit firing into the unseen cloud that loomed before us and started to fire at the tops of the siege towers. After several tries, I succeeded in striking one and as the other had, it went up into flames. I could hear John cheering behind me and I got caught up in what John affectionately called "the eye of the tiger". It was no longer a matter of who was right or wrong. It was a matter of who lived and who died. There wasn't a second place in survival. It was winner take all.

The outskirts of the smoke cloud began to pour onto us and I knew it wouldn't be long before we would be face to face with our enemy. If they managed to get past the barrier of our fence line we would surely lose what little of our dream that had not already been destroyed. I stopped firing as a ghostlike silence gripped the battlefield. Their bullets stopped firing and their siege machines stopped creaking forward and for a moment, in the haze, the morning appeared as nothing more than to be draped in a quiet fog.

Shattering the silence, as a hammer would glass, blood-curdling screams screeched from the hanging smoke, enveloping us in a tidal wave of fear. Scores of Chassers dressed in bright red ceremonial war gear, came running out of the thick black smoke and tried to scale our fenced in perimeter. The poor creatures didn't understand the power of electricity because they hit it hard and in huge numbers. The smell of burning flesh filled my nasal cavities and nearly caused me to vomit from the horrid stench. Seeing the poor creatures stuck to the fence and frying like slabs of meat was almost more than I could bear to watch. John knew if they continued to pile up on our fence they might over load it, shorting it out. Quickly, he jumped over his bunker's wall and cut the power to the fence just long enough for its victims to fall to the ground. Then he charged it up again catching a whole new group of attackers. He did this several times, reminding me of watching an energized bug trap on a hot summer night. After nearly a dozen failed attempts to scale our electric wall, those that were still alive pulled back into the smoke and disappeared.

At first glance it appeared they were retreating and in excitement I nearly cheered, but I refrained as I noticed their towers moving toward us again. The two that John and I had hit earlier had finally collapsed into ashes, but ten more were still rolling.

"Everybody, concentrate your fire on those towers!" yelled John observantly.

He got Cynthia to take his place at the gate's power switch, ran over to the gate and started to fire at the towers. I stepped up next to John and we began to focus our fire on one tower at a time until it erupted into flame. Before long, we had ignited six out of the ten and were working on another when I heard a cry from Jenna.

"Oh my god, Edmund!" she screamed.

I could see her holding him in her arms crying and I began to run to his aid when John's large hand stopped me cold.

"There is nothing you can do for him."

I struggled to break free of his hold, but his grip was like steel.

"Let Cynthia help him," he said gritting his teeth, "I need you here."

His eyes flared with commanding fortitude. I bit down on my upper lip and stood next to him firing my rifle. In firing on the rolling towers, we managed to put down two more before they reached our perimeter.

Their towers were innovative and had an extensive pulley system. As soon as they got within range of our walls, a platform flipped over unfolding into a ramp. Two managed to do so and, within seconds, dozens of Chassers were inside the compound. John discarded his rifle, took position in front of the nearest ramp and engaged the assaulters at pointblank range with his energy pistol. He began to shoot them like he was in a turkey shoot, melting the faces of those unfortunate enough to step from the tower in front of him, but looking out through the fence I could see more Chassers lined up to enter the attacking siege towers. We would not be able to outlast their superior numbers and I knew they would overrun us, unless we disabled their towers.

John was doing his part by stopping the flow of the enemy from the first tower, but more were pouring in from the second. Once they were inside, they began to take defensive positions behind our buildings and fire their strange wrist slings. Several shots whizzed past me forcing me to run for cover. I began to sprint back toward the bunker nearest the second tower, in hopes of getting a good firing position, when I took a hit directly behind my left knee and collapsed to the ground. Several more shots struck the ground around me, persuading me to make a desperate crawl to safety. Unbelievably, I made the bunker without being hit a second time and quickly began to fire on the second tower, hoping to stop its flow of Chassers.

My first beam shot up into its entrance and hit two Chassers causing them to fall backwards down the long chute on the other side of our fence. My second energy beam caught the face of the tower below its entrance and in several seconds a small flame engulfed the front of it. Surprisingly, several more Chassers fearlessly leaped through the growing flames to get inside our compound before the tower was completely consumed. Small metal missiles ricocheted off the wall in front of me spiraling chucks of rock into my body forcefully knocking me on my back. I raised my rifle over the edge of my bunker and made a few blind shots, in hopes of discouraging any type of assault upon my position. I looked back toward John and noticed that the rest of our group had managed to disable the last siege tower and watched in amazement as John handled the rest of the Chassers that had infiltrated our perimeter. The Chassers are not a small or weak species by any means, but I watched John encounter them in hand to hand combat thrashing them around as if they were rag dolls.

After a few moments, the suppressive fire I had been encountering quit altogether and John and I policed the rest of our compound easily dispatching those we found with our technically superior weapons. It wasn't until we had cleared out the last of the Chassers that I noticed the wounds that John had sustained in his valiant defense of our compound. His body was covered in large red welts from the impact of the many sling-like bullets he had suffered in all the commotion of our defense. When I first saw them I found myself at a loss for words. I couldn't understand how a man could take such punishment without showing any signs of pain. I had been hit with just one of their shots and knew very well the impact they delivered and yet John stood and took a dozen or more and never collapsed.

"That was good work over there," he said pointing toward the burnt tower to the south of our compound.

"Thanks," I replied softly, knowing very well it had been he who had saved us.

We walked over to the fence to examine the damage dealt to those who had been foolish enough to try and scale its electric structure. Burnt black flesh covered their bodies leaving wide-open oozing flesh wounds. With their tusks and scorched skin, they looked somewhat like a roasted pigs.

"Something smells like bacon," said John heartlessly sniffing the air.

Cynthia came running down the small hill that housed her bunker and embraced John. She began to cry as she held him, embarrassing him. I walked off to leave them in peace, ignoring an embarrassment that I would have relished.

# Chapter 11

W e spent the rest of the evening and the next day recovering from the assault placed upon us by our newest neighbors and enemies. No one had been seriously hurt, including Edmund, who had been knocked unconscious by a direct blow to the head and fortunately had only suffered a light concussion. It was now obvious to us that we would not be able to live in peace with our neighbors and that something had to be done soon if we were going to survive.

Being a democracy, our first action was to hold another meeting and once again our leader, Dr. Kineard, was not in attendance. I could tell by her mannerisms that Cynthia was very concerned about his well being and that any comment about his lack of attendance would have been greeted with her disapproval. He was a patient under her care and therefore exempt from questions about his actions. Although I wasn't a human psychiatrist, I believed that the discovery of his wife's murder had sent him into a state of psychosis. With the absence of Dr. Kineard, Edmund, with a grave look on his face, opened the meeting.

"I believe all of us can agree after what happened yesterday, that something has to be done about our current situation."

"I think it's pretty clear what has to be done," said John leaning back in his chair. "We have to find out where these Chassers live and eliminate them."

"What?" replied Edmund in absolute disbelief. "Surely you don't think that a group of five could eradicate a tribe or nation of beings."

"We just kicked the shit out of an entire army without taking a single causality. If we attack now while they are broken, we can finish them off before they know what hit them."

"How could we do such a thing?" Edmund asked curiously.

"You brainy types are killing me. You're telling me, in a room full of doctors, I am going to have to bring up that the ship we rode here in is nuclear."

"Are you talking about the radioactive materials from our ship's engines?" asked Edmund.

"Why yes I am Edmund, unless you know of some other nuclear device," said John callously.

"Wait a minute," interrupted Jenna quickly. "I hate these things as much or more than any of you, but I don't want to completely destroy them."

"Why not Jenna?" responded John. "They want to destroy you."

"I know John," I replied, "but I didn't come across light years of space to invade a planet and perform genocide upon its inhabitants."

"I think we all know why you came across lights years of space," countered John with his arms folded across his chest.

The entire room got caught in a black hole of silence. His response threw me for a loop and left me utterly speechless. I could see the awkward looks on everyone's faces and I believe even John was sorry that he had brought up my past with Anne. After several lingering seconds of silence, Edmund spoke and cut the silence around us like a knife.

"John, what you are proposing could be catastrophic, not only to the Chassers, but to us as well," he said. "And I can't even begin to explain the possible consequences to our surrounding environment."

"What about the consequences of another attack by those things?" replied John angrily. "No one in the history of mankind or alien has ever won a completely defensive war. Eventually the enemy will adapt to our defenses and discover a way to overcome them."

He stood up and pounded the table actually lifting it off the ground with his massive fist.

"At some point you have to attack to eliminate the threat before it eliminates you and the only way we can do that is with a nuclear attack!"

"John," I said, "the only reason any of us is still here is because of your actions yesterday, but I can't go along with your plan to simply wipe them out like they are some kind of pest. This is their planet, we are the aliens here and it wouldn't be right for us to blow them off of it."

"What other choice do we have?" replied John throwing up his hands.

"We could leave," said Jenna quietly.

"You have got to be kidding!" screamed John. "After everything we have been through, I can't believe you just said that! Not only has one of us died and another one gone completely insane, but one of us actually turned into a murderous bitch, who is running around doing who knows what, and you want to just give up?"

Edmund solemnly responded, "I think after everything that has happened going home may be what's in the best interest of everyone involved."

I could see the look of disgust on everyone's face, but in no one's was it as evident as it was in John's. I knew part of it was his unwillingness to give up, but there was much more to it than that. I believe that he, as well as the rest of us, had begun to feel a sort of cohesiveness as a group, even as dysfunctional as we had been. John, completely exasperated with the situation, didn't say another word and our future came to a vote. The vote, with Dr. Kineard absent, was four for leaving and one to stay. After seeing the result John got up and left in frustration, while the rest of us looked at each other in disbelief. It took several minutes for the realization that it was finally over to grasp the four of us in the room. Lives had been thrown away and years wasted with nothing to show for it. I continued to admire Cynthia's independence, as she was able to sit by her husband and vote against him to stay true to her own principles.

It was decided that we should leave as early as possible to avoid another attack and everyone left to prepare for the long trip back. I couldn't believe it was going to be over. The entire trip had been a bust and I couldn't help but feel responsible. I do believe the group would have encountered the Chassers had Anne and I not come, but I couldn't help thinking that maybe they would have weathered the situation far better. Everyone decided to work through the rest of the day and night, so that we could leave early the next morning. A multitude of questions swarmed through my head as I went back to my room and began to pack. What would it be like back home once we returned nearly a hundred years later? Would we be looked upon as complete failures or would we have already been long forgotten? And what of Anne, were we going to leave her alone on this planet with no way of getting back?

I could hear John outside in the compound loading up the ground track. Even as angry as he was, he was still outside loading equipment at the will of our now defunct society. Besides my writings and a few other personal belongings, I decided to leave most of my possessions on Hipparchus II along with my heart. What did I really need for a forty seven year nap? I threw my pack over my shoulder and turned around to head outside when I was stopped in my tracks by shock. Standing in front of me with wild flowing hair was Anne, holding a pistol with her finger tensely wrapped around its trigger.

"You finally managed to screw everything up, didn't you?" she said in delirium.

I could see from her mannerisms that she was in a state of psychosis.

"Please Anne calm down." I said reassuringly, realizing that one reflex in her finger would end my life. "Don't do anything irrational."

"I think killing you would be the only rational thing to do, wouldn't you? Considering you destroyed my life!" she said shaking her pistol at me in rhythm with her speech.

"Anne," I said gently.

"Shut up!" she said interrupting me. "Just shut up! What the hell are you doing with that bag uh? Are you going somewhere?"

I could tell from her current state of mind that anything I said was only going to provoke her so I stood in front of her without speaking.

"So," she asked angrily, "everyone has decided to leave poor old Anne here alone to take care of herself? What about my innocent baby, were you going to leave it too... huh? Did you think of that or were all of you just thinking about yourselves and your stupid society?"

"Anne!" said Dr. Kineard's deep voice.

Anne spun around and behind her in the doorway stood her mentor, holding an energy pistol of his own.

"Charles dear," she said while straightening her messy and tattered hair. "I know what you are thinking, but we can work this out."

Although she had turned to speak with Dr. Kineard, she continued to point her pistol at me, leaving me helpless.

"Work what out Anne?" he said acerbically. "Are we going to resurrect Jane and restore my respect with everyone here?"

"No," she said nervously, "they're leaving. We can stay and start over... you, me and our baby."

"My god no," he said lowering his pistol to his side. "What have I done?"

"Oh, it will be wonderful!" she said gleefully rushing over and embracing him. "The three of us together forever, just as I have always dreamed!

Afraid of what she might do if I tried to grab her with a pistol in her hand I stood helpless.

"We will be alone," she said quickly whispering into his ear. "We can continue on with your work without fear of anyone bothering us. I promise I will make you happy again. Just like when we were together. It was so special. It's never been like that with anyone."

"I had never been with anyone but Jane before you," he said lifelessly.

She rose up and began to kiss him on his neck, and after dropping her pistol, began to caress his body. When she dropped her gun, I saw the opportunity to seize her, but before I could act a blast came from Dr. Kineard's pistol and Anne fell to the floor holding her chest. She rolled over onto her back and I could see a gaping hole in her chest exposing her burnt bones and organs. Not even the capable Cynthia could save her now. She died quickly, leaving Dr. Kineard and I alone in my room. We both stared at her body and although beautiful, I think we were both relieved that she was finally dead. Dr. Kineard lifted up his pistol as if in a trance and put it into his mouth.

"No!" I screamed diving toward him.

His pistol went off in a flash and I ended up tackling a dead man. Lying on top of him, I looked up at where he face should have been, but found it had been burned off at his neck. I hastily rolled off of him and began to vomit in the corner. It was an atrocious sight of burnt flesh, bone and brain that I will never forget. In a few moments, both Edmund and Jenna came to see what I was screaming about and stepped back in horror at the bloody sight. This time the burials were not modern ones of space, such as Jane's, but were like those of our ancient past, where we placed their bodies in the soil. Only Edmund spoke at the funeral and he spoke only a few words.

"Here lies Dr. Charles Kineard, a great scientist and brilliant visionary. May his body and soul rest where he dreamed such a beautiful dream," he said with a lowered head.

Nothing else was said about Anne whom we buried just a few feet away. It was a sad ending to a hopeful beginning.

After the funeral, Cynthia begged me to take a sedative, afraid of what I might do, but I refused and left to be alone. We were down to five now and I was the only one left that stunk of the conspiracy that had nearly destroyed us.

I had nothing left to live for, as my work would suffer from the scandal. Who would want to read the psychological ramblings of a man who was certainly going to be considered mentally unstable at best? I began to wrestle with my options as the rest of the group continued to prepare for our long trip home. The only real choices I had, save ending my life like Dr. Kineard, was to either go back to a world where I no longer knew anyone or to stay on this tiny moon alone. At least here, I wouldn't have to suffer humiliation in front of my peers or try to start over, but the idea of staying here on this planet with its hostile natives was farfetched, to say the least.

Jenna asked me to help pack up her and Edmund's equipment, as a kind gesture, and I accepted in hopes of forgetting my problems, if only for a little while. While Cynthia, Jenna and I prepared the last load, John and Edmund left with the ground track to prepare our ship for its launch the next morning. Since we were leaving in such haste, most of our equipment was actually going to be left behind, kind of like a grave marking of a failed society.

Once everything was packed and ready to go, I sat at the edge of our compound and waited for Edmund and John's return. The beautiful scenery of this tiny moon still amazed me and I wondered how long it would be before every trace of our having been here would be gone. It would be as it had been before we came. It would continue to circle the giant planet Oniesis, while its inhabitants, the Alutas and Chassers, struggled with each other for dominance and survival.

## Intergalactic Eden

It was nearly three hours before they returned and from Edmund's face I could tell something had gone wrong. He stepped down with a long gaunt face and looked into our waiting eyes.

"They have completely destroyed our ship," he said gravely.

# Cosmic Contemplations

# Chapter 12

Edmund explained that the Chassers had destroyed everything possible, not a light had been left unbroken and not a wire uncut. Then after gutting the inside, as someone would a pumpkin, they burned it to the ground to leave nothing salvageable. Fortunately, the fire had not been fervent enough to compromise the internal components of the engine or its materials, which were enclosed in a thick fire resistant casing to prevent an explosion from entering the ship in case of catastrophic engine failure. By attacking us and destroying our only escape, they had forced us into a war of survival. Whether he was happy about it or not, John was going to get his war with the dreaded Chassers. Edmund, who seemed to slowly but surely be taking charge of our group, called another meeting. When John heard that there was going to be another emergency meeting, he made the remark of: "Have we ever had any other kind?"

"As I am sure by now, everyone understands our latest dilemma and the consequences of the decision that we as a group must make," said Edmund dolefully.

"Please don't tell me that someone here has found a way to cower and hide from these savages," said John.

No one said a word. John stood up and walked in front of us as if he was a schoolteacher and we were his eager students.

"I have stood by, listened and even carried out this group's decision from day one, but this time I am the expert. No one in this room has the military qualifications that I do and no one is more qualified in regard to war than I. Military operations never work under the rule of a committee, that is why all successful armed forces have always been under the command of one leader. This is not a test tube or an experiment… this is utter survival. If we do not remove this enemy, they will remove us. They attacked us and destroyed our ship for one reason and one reason alone. They want blood and we are going to give it to them!" he said forcefully. "What I am asking for is complete and unquestioned support from this group. I know you brainy types like to question everything until it turns blue, but second guessing or indecisive action during a campaign will leave us all dead with no one left to bury us as we did our companions."

With his speech on our minds and a unanimous vote to declare war on our new enemies on our lips, our dream of starting a peaceful society with a clean slate ended. We were to be a community of war and destruction as our fathers' had been, since the dawn of time. It seemed no matter how educated or civilized man became he still couldn't escape his primal desire to make war and commit atrocities in the name of his own best interest.

I left our meeting room with a sick feeling and ashamed to be of the species Homo sapiens. John zealously began to organize his newly recruited soldiers and so began our operation against the Chassers. Edmund and Jenna, the last two scientists in our group, were given the task of creating a bomb while the rest of us prepared the compound for another possible attack. Both Edmund and Jenna were out of their field when it came to nuclear science and I could tell from Edmund's face it was wearing on him.

We worked from dusk till dawn every day and except, for Edmund or Jenna, we spent most of our nights on guard duty as well. Although Edmund and Jenna were exempt from the long nights of guard duty, I didn't envy them in the slightest. Both worked around the clock on a subject neither really understood nor enjoyed. Nearly a week had passed when late one night, after I had completed one of my many guard shifts Edmund came to see me in my quarters.

"Alex," he said poking his head in the door, "do you have a moment?"

"Edmund, I have eternity," I said holding out my arms out and throwing my gear onto the bed. "Come on in."

I collapsed on my bed as he walked by and sat in a chair across from me.

"I need to get something off my mind," he said, hanging his head while stroking the short red strands on top of it as if trying to pull them out.

"Edmund, I don't really think I am the best person in whom you should confide. Actually, I'm considering giving up psychiatry all together. I just don't have what it takes," I said in exasperation.

"Alex, I want to talk to you because you are my friend," he said kindly, "and one bad decision doesn't mean you are unqualified in your field. Hell, if that were true we wouldn't have one practicing doctor or scientist in the universe."

"Thanks for stroking my ego, doctor."

"You are welcome doctor," he said laughing softly.

It was a joke between the two of us to call each other doctor with each sentence. It always lightened up the situation.

"It's this bomb I am working on," he said pausing, "I am out of my league. If only Dr. Kineard or Anne were here."

"Please don't mention those two names," I said covering up my face. "I don't think it would be any better if those two were still here."

"I meant for their expertise in chemistry."

"Well, I failed math, so you are talking to the wrong guy."

"I have to start all over and relearn the basics," he said. "This isn't a graduate thesis I am working on here, Alex."

"So what you are saying is that this place could turn into a yellow mushroom any minute?" I asked.

"No," he said crossly, "I became a botanist to study life and to nurture it. Not to blow it up."

"So you are struggling with it ethically?" I asked sitting up.

"That's the psychiatrist I know and love."

"Well?" I asked again.

"I can do it. I just don't know if I want to. I mean, I know it has to be done, but it's different when you have to personally make the decision. It's different when you're responsible for the deaths of thousands."

"He is right, you know," I said bluntly.

"Who?"

"John," I said shortly, "he's right... it's the only choice we have if we want to survive. He doesn't approach things from an ethical standpoint. He looks at it purely with the desire to survive. To

91

him any means are justified if survival is the end result. You are our leader now all of our lives are in your hands."

He sat silent with his face in his hands and didn't move.

"I wish I could be more help, Edmund, but this is your decision."

A long block of silence passed, before he finally left my room. I knew what his decision was going to be, but I also knew he would struggle with it for the rest of his life.

The next morning the bomb was complete, as I knew it would be. Edmund had obviously already finished it before we had our talk last night and was just struggling with the consequences of his actions. John was enthused now that the tide had turned in our war effort against the Chassers and was ready to deliver a knockout blow before they could regroup and mass another assault. Actually, the only thing that surprised me that morning was that John intended to personally take the bomb and set it off himself! When I found out his plans I immediately confronted him.

"Have you lost your mind?" I yelled at him.

"What the hell is that supposed to mean?" he replied angrily, clenching his fist.

"Edmund just told me that you are going to take the bomb and set it off yourself," I said standing my ground against his commanding figure.

"How did you think we were going to deliver it?" he asked sarcastically. "Put it in a wooden horse and have them come get it?"

"We have remote control surveillance tracks that can be modified to transport it," I replied.

"Hmm…and what if one of their patrols finds it before it reaches its destination? Or even better, it malfunctions? Then what the hell are we going to do? This is the only bomb we got, meaning it's the one chance we got to defeat these things and I am not letting our lives depend on one of those electronic toys!" he said smartly. "If this bomb does not go off in the right place, then we are going to learn an awful lot about these Alutas you like so much, because we are going to have to live like them to survive."

"John," I said gently in an attempt to reason with him, "there has to be another way."

"I appreciate what you are trying to do, Alex," he said with his hand on my shoulder, "but this is the only way. I have to ensure it is done right."

"Let me do it," I pleaded. "You have so much more to lose than I. My god, you have Cynthia to think about!"

"Cynthia is exactly why I am doing this," he said loudly. "Don't take this personally Alex, but I don't want our lives in your hands."

"Then I am going with you," I said forcefully.

He turned around and looked at me as if he had taken what I said to him personally.

"No you're not," he said coldly.

"I should be doing this, not you. At least let me help you."

"I am going to have enough to worry about without having to baby-sit you. That's it, end of discussion," he said walking away.

A fury rose from within me. I was tired of being ostracized and considered useless, for one mistake. Edmund was right. One mistake shouldn't disable one's viability in a profession or society. I could still be an asset to our group and that was exactly what I was going to do.

I quickly took up with Edmund and Jenna to have a quick look at the bomb. It wasn't very big, just a little smaller than an average person's head, but much heavier than it appeared. I acted as if I was interested in how they had completed it and got a full explanation of its mechanics and operation. Edmund told me everything in detail, almost as if he was proud of the bomb as a scientific accomplishment. It had been equipped with two manual switches. The blue one activated a timer, so it could be set and left to explode. The bright red one, in case of dire consequences, caused instant detonation. Clear thick plastic casings covered the switches to avert accidental armament.

"How long is the timer?" I asked Edmund.

"Twenty four hours," he replied. "Long enough for John to get well out of the range of the initial explosion and to escape any aftereffects of its fall out."

"Twenty four hours?" I asked unbelievably. "Don't you think they might discover it before it detonates?"

"I doubt it," he said walking over to another table. "This baby packs a wallop. He won't have to set it in the middle of them. All

John has to do is get it near their city or base, whatever it may be, and bury it just below the ground."

"And bang," I said lightly.

"Yeah, and bang," he said sadly.

"When is he going to do it?" I asked curiously.

"He leaves tomorrow morning," he answered. "We can monitor its detonation through Corvus. Once it's done we should not have to worry about any more threats from the Chassers and we can try and rebuild."

"Well," I said, "I'm going to get some sleep since I am going to be pulling a double on guard shift tonight."

"Since I've finished my work, I would be glad to split the duty with you tonight."

"Nah… I kind of enjoy watching us spin around Oniesis at night. It is a beautiful sight, but if I get tired I'll come get you."

"Okay," he replied simply, "I'll either be in here or my room if you need me."

"Surely you are not going to stay up all night with your bomb again?" I asked him quickly in hopes of deterring such an action.

"I'm just going to run a few more test on the timer and double check all the connections again," he said while taking off the bomb's outer casing. "I want to make sure everything goes as planned."

"Goodnight, Edmund, try to get some rest."

He nodded to reassure me and I left him alone to audit his work. I walked down the hall and unlocked the door to our second storage room. John had recently converted it into an armory and I quickly found everything I would need for my impending trip. I took my post for guard duty and waited for my chance to sneak out with the bomb. It seemed everyone was having a difficult time sleeping and nearly half the night had passed before everyone, except Edmund, finally fell asleep. I sat in the cold night atop our barn watching Edmund's lab, but its light never ceased. I knew if he didn't go to sleep soon, I would have to do something drastic, so I could be long gone before anyone noticed the bomb missing the next morning. After another full hour passed and Edmund showed no signs of letting up, I climbed down from my post and went to take matters into my own hands.

Through the frosted glass in the lab door window, I could see the shadow of his body working diligently on his bomb. I slowly turned the door's handle and crept in behind him. The door made a slight creak and he turned around startled.

"You scared the shit out of me," he said relieved. "You should really knock first, especially so late at night."

I didn't answer him but slowing began to knot up a long rope I had brought with me. After I didn't respond, he quit his work and turned toward me again. He looked into my eyes and although I don't think he knew at that moment what I was planning to do, he knew something wasn't right.

"Alex," he said backing away from me, "what are you doing?"

I locked the lab door, pulled out a rope and began to walk toward him. He scrambled behind one of his lab tables and pushed it between us, knocking over several objects, exploding them on the floor. I quickly took hold of the table's other side to quiet it.

"Don't make this any harder on me than it already is Edmund," I said while struggling with the table. "I don't want to hurt you, I just want the bomb."

Not saying another word, he leaned back against the wall and used his feet to shove the table into me, knocking me down before making a run for the door. I managed to get a firm grip on his ankle as he passed, using it to pull him to the floor. I crawled onto his back and held him down with my knees quickly binding his struggling limbs.

Once I had finished binding and gagging him, I tried to make him as comfortable as possible and went over to get the bomb.

"I am sorry about this, Edmund. The last thing I wanted to do was fight with you," I said to him sorrowfully, not daring to look into his eyes. "I hope you don't hold it against me."

Fortunately, our scuffle didn't alarm anyone in the compound and I was beyond our compound's gates within ten minutes and off into the night.

# Cosmic Contemplations

# Chapter 13

I Hurried off toward where John and I had first encountered the Chassers and put as much space between our compound and myself as I could before light. I walked on through the night enjoying what might be the last trip I would ever take. Once the light of our moon's two suns reached me, I found myself surrounded once again in a world of astounding beauty. Everything was alive! The swirling wind and flowers danced around me as a crowd would a hero in a parade. I traversed one nearly endless flowing green field after another on my quest to deliver death and saw nothing of life, save the elements of nature.

That night I took refuge from the wet winds of Hipparchus II and slept for only a short while. I began the second day of my journey when it was still dark and pondered what was happening back at our compound. I knew Edmund would be quick to forgive me, but John would not be as quick to do so. He was probably fuming the morning he found the bomb and I gone and I was glad I wouldn't have to see his temper in action.

On the third day of my trip, I finally lost sight of the long blue surface of Jenna's Lake and found myself immersed in the thick underbrush of Hipparchus' forest. Curious, I took out the heavy object that pounded against my back and held it up to get a better look at it, pondering how something could contain so much hope and destruction at the same time. It was hard to comprehend the massive destructive power that was bottled up in such a small round shiny ball. We would not be the first men to use such destruction against an unsuspecting foe and unfortunately not the last.

I stood up and had just finished rewrapping it when I heard something coming through the brush behind me. I quickly put the bomb in my backpack, pulled my pistol from its holster and kneeled down. My ears strained to make out from which direction the sounds came. My fingers were soaked in perspiration as they gripped the trigger on my pistol waiting tensely before the swaying bushes. A tall slender being slipped out of the brush before me and froze upon seeing me. It was Hummer! He still had our restraint collar around his neck. I lowered my pistol and put out my other hand to show I meant him no harm. I know he recognized me, because he reached up with his hand and touched his mouth, an action he always did when we spoke, as if trying to make his mouth move in a better attempt to mock my speech. I was pleased to see him alive and finally, after a few moments of dead silence between us, I took one step. It startled him and he took off through the brush. I tried to follow, but I eventually ended up standing in the brush pulling thorns out of my clothing for the trouble. Every form of life has at least one aspect about itself that allows it the ability to overcome all odds and survive, whether it is intelligence, fertility or adaptability, and Hummer's species' was flight.

I traveled four more days without incident, except for sighting one strange natural wonder after another. Edmund had explained to me how different planetary rotations and gravitational pulls affected vegetation and natural formations. I saw immense trees whose trunks were twisted into knots and long smooth rocks that stretched for miles polished to a glossy shine by the eternal abrasive wet winds of Hipparchus II.

Although I had already traveled further than our first contact with the Chassers, I had not seen a single sign of their existence. I could only hope that their community was large enough or apparent enough that I would not accidentally pass it up. With each step I began to second guess my decision to take on such an enormous task on my own. A new fear took hold of me, not the fear one experiences for his life, but the sinking fear of catastrophic failure. If I failed or didn't find the Chassers before they attacked our compound, all would be lost.

Two more days passed without a sign of my destination and alternate scenarios began to play out in my mind. What if they had already assaulted our compound and destroyed everyone leaving me alone on a distant planet or the detonation of our bomb failed to destroy them?

Another day passed and I finally cleared the thick forest I had been in for so many days. Before me stretched a field that raced off into the distance finally ending at the beginning of a large mountain chain. Its sight, although breathtaking, sank my heart, for I knew how difficult it would be for me to traverse those mountains and how easily I could pass an entire city in an adjacent valley and never see it. I turned around and looked back to ponder if I should backtrack to make sure I had not missed them when I saw Hummer again. His tall thin black form stood motionless, observing me, outside the tree line of the woods I had left. I knew any attempt to contact him would cause him to flee so I made a waving gesture at him and continued on toward the towering mountains ahead.

It took me nearly an entire day to cross that long field and at every stop I made, my curious friend Hummer was still with me, following me step for step, never letting the distance between us diminish. It was near dusk when the terrain began to harden from the soft field behind me to the rough rocks of the mountains ahead. I found a small hillside to make camp under and ate some of the fruit that Edmund grew so well. He knew his business when it came to plants, satisfying their required nutrients and stimuli, which meant his produce was lush. I took several bites and had sat back to rest for what would surely be a difficult journey tomorrow, when Hummer came up to the edge of my campsite and crouched across from me. I knew what he wanted, but I wasn't going to make it easy for him. I sat down a piece of fruit, a few feet away, and continued to eat mine acting as if his presence meant nothing. I could see that coming so close to me made him uneasy, but he crawled over to the fruit and snatched it up, never taking his eyes off of me. I laughed as he grabbed the fruit, startling him, and causing him to fall over backwards. I began to laugh louder and once he saw I wasn't going to try to grab him, he settled down and touched his lips, trying to mimic my laughs. He devoured his fruit as if he was in a race and we repeated the same scenario two more times before I decided to stop squandering my food supplies. I knew he could find food easier on this planet than I. I began to speak to him, as I had when he was in our captivity, in hopes of continuing to breech our differences, when he suddenly turned his head and jumped off into the night. I wondered if

I had done something to spook him, when I heard the sounds of rocks sliding. I jumped up and after finding a good hiding spot gripped my pistol tight. The sound of rocks sliding continued to get louder before I heard a different, but far more terrifying sound. It was the unmistakable sound of a Chasser's grunt, as I had heard it so often in our encounters. I did not look up to try to see where or how many there were, for fear of being seen.

Although it had cooled off with the disappearance of the suns, I began to sweat profusely as my enemy moved closer. My hands turned white from gripping my pistol and my eyes swelled open as I peered through the brush. Through the shrubbery, I could see a Chasser roaming through my camp examining the fruit cores I had foolishly left behind. Two more appeared and I knew that it was only a matter of time before they would begin to comb the area in search of me. If I ran they would certainly catch me. I knew what I had to do to survive and that meant eliminate the enemy. So I heeded the lesson John taught me so well and took the hunt to them.

I stood up and fired into the one closest to me and dropped the creature in two shots. The other two turned toward me and I dropped another before he could react. The third one fired his wrist sling, wounding me, but not before I got another shot off sending it spinning to the ground. His shot hit me directly in the chest knocking me onto my back. For a moment, my chest hardened and I couldn't breathe. I gasped for air rising to a sitting position ripping off my shirt. The projectile had penetrated the skin and lodged between my ribs. Half of it was protruding out like a round fishing weight and I tried to get a grip on it, but it was wedged in too tightly.

Another shot whizzed by my head and ricocheted off the hillside behind me. I turned to see if it was one of the Chassers I had shot, but all three bodies were still lying on the ground motionless. I rolled behind a rock and looked to see from where the shots were coming. Several more zinged past my position and one glanced off the rock in front of me, sending shards of broken rock into my face. I covered my face with my hands and when I pulled them down they were covered in blood. I couldn't tell from where the shots were coming or if from more than one position. I heard something moving along the rocky ledge above me, just before a shot bounced near my leg. I caught a quick glimpse of him moving along the ledge to get a better shot at my flank. I jumped up and made a run for a large rock. I saw him rise up and fire, but the shot flew by me harmlessly and I took position behind a rock below the small cliff.

As far as I could tell there was only one Chasser and I had to make sure he didn't leave alive. I waited quietly for several minutes, listening for movement. A few rocks bounced down from above me and I could tell from the dust boiling up he was moving quickly. I stood up to take a shot, but he got over the hill above me before I could pull the trigger. Seeing him run, I did what the Chassers did so well and became the hunter. I ran up the hillside as fast as I could so as not to lose sight of him for long. Once I made the top, I stopped and began searching for movement. I didn't notice anything, not even a swinging branch or speck of floating dust to give me a hint what direction he had fled. I stood still and cursed my failure. He had gotten away and before long they would be out in numbers looking for me. I gripped my throbbing chest and kneeled down in pain.

A small rock trickled by me and I spun around just in time to shove the Chasser's arm away. His arm sling fired off into the distance and I put my pistol into his chest. He seized my arm pushing it away, gnashing at my face with his tusk as we tumbled down the hill into the woods below. I fired my gun as we fell and lost hold of him as we crashed through the brush. Sharp branches tore my clothing as I plunged through the foliage, while the skin on my hands shed free as I tried to grip at them to slow myself down. My descent through the brush came to a rolling stop in a flat depression and, after getting to my feet, I found my adversary dead from a gunshot through the neck.

In an attempt to hide my presence from the Chassers, I hid the bodies and moved on through the dark night. I found a small trail that they had apparently used to move up into my camp and felt pretty sure that it would lead me to something. I had not gone far when I heard a quick beeping noise. I instinctively rolled off the trail and took a prone firing position. Darkness, along with an eerie silence, was all around me. Even if there was something out there in the dark, I would not be able to see it until it was on top of me. My breathing from the scuffle near the cliffs was still prominent and I tried to quiet it down so not to give away my position. Another beep swelled into my ears and my heart froze! My god, the beep had come from my backpack! I ripped it off my shoulders and in a panic jerked it open. I pulled out the small silver ball and a blue light was flashing on it. The clear casing that covered the blue switch had shattered exposing the switch. My fall had triggered the twenty four hour delay switch!

The blue light illuminated my face as I sat looking at it in disgust. If it had been the red switch I would have evaporated before I knew what had happened. Knowing nothing about its mechanical makeup and being too far away from our compound for Edmund to disarm it, gave me few options. I wrapped it up, put it back in my pack and jumped to my feet, desperately running down the path ahead. I reached up and held my chest as I ran. Blood was seeping around the sling bullet lodged in my chest and had soaked my shirt down to my waist, but I ran on frantically in a near stupor.

I only had twenty four hours to find the Chassers and I had no idea in which direction to go. As I ran through the darkness thoughts hurled through my head. I feared so greatly that I might once again fail everyone. Unfortunately, for all of us, John was going to be right about not wanting to trust our society to me. There was nothing left for me to do, but hope I would find the enemy before I collapsed and our bomb detonated. Either way, I had become a kamikaze. Even if I did find the Chassers quickly, I probably would not have enough time to escape the bomb's blast. The worst thing of all would be for me not to find them and to disappear with our only hope.

I ran on through the night till morning and finally fell in exhaustion as my legs gave away. I tumbled to the ground collapsing hard rolling against a tree and banging my head against its trunk. I tried to get up and although my mind had the will, my body was too weak to carry on. The bright morning light gave way to a darkening sheet that seemed to fall over my eyes. Disorientation overcame my conscious and I tried to support myself by leaning up against a tree, but collapsed into darkness.

When I came to, it was still light. I arose to a sitting position in a sweat from the heat around me and calmly looked around as I regained my senses. A gentle wind quietly blew the leaves around in a serene dance that was being held for my benefit alone. Suddenly, the seriousness of my situation hit me like a ton of bricks and I leaped to my feet. How long had I been out and how much longer did I have till I became only a memory? The first sun of Hipparchus II was nearing the top of the sky, meaning it was about midday, but of which day? Had I been unconscious overnight or for just a few hours? Did I have seventeen hours or seventeen minutes left before detonation?

## Intergalactic Eden

I began to run hysterically toward the only hope I had, the small trail that stretched through the thick forest. As I ran, I began to dispose of everything that wasn't pertinent to my desperate mission. I threw all my food and equipment to the wayside, keeping only my empty pack, the bomb and my pistol. The act lightened my load, but I was unable to shed my condition. It was weighing on me heavily and I wasn't sure how much longer I could keep up such a frantic pace. My surroundings melted into a blur as my legs carried me quickly through the forest. The shadows of the surrounding trees and the leaves below my feet merged into one long streak creating a hypnotic aura around my frantic run. Suddenly, I slammed into a dark fuzzy object. It hit me squarely in my chest and sent my legs flying out from under me. I hit the ground hard and in a panic pulled out my pistol. A foot kicked it from my hand and sent it airborne.

"There you are you little shit!" said the voice angrily.

I looked up and towering above me was the commanding stature of John.

# Cosmic Contemplations

# Chapter 14

He looked down at me like a disappointed father would a disobedient son. I tried to get up but he kicked my side, catching me flush along my ribs stealing my breath.

"I ought to kill you for this!" he said.

I tried to get up again, but he shoved me down with the sole of his foot again exerting his dominance.

"Stay down there before I decide to get rough with you," he ordered.

I tried to respond, but could do nothing but struggle for air.

"I found your little shoot out back there," he said. "Not too bad for a civilian."

"John!" I said forcing out my words coughing. "The bomb has been activated."

He stood silent for a moment.

"What?" he asked stunned. "For how long?"

"I'm not sure," I said gasping.

"What do you mean you're not sure?" he yelled. "How the hell could you not know?"

"I lost consciousness," I replied with my head down.

"Okay," he said trying to calm down, "about how long do you think it has been?"

"I don't know."

"This is just fucking great!" he yelled at the top of his lungs, while kicking a large branch off a tree. "Any minute we are going to be turned into shadows and all you can say is I don't know! Let me tell you something... that is not good enough! "

He reached down and lifted me off the ground like a child ripping my backpack off my back. He pulled out the bomb and unwrapped it as if there might be some distant hope that I was wrong. A flashing blue light confirmed our situation and he turned to me.

"You finally managed to fuck up everything," he said angrily. "Coming out here with Anne and ruining our lives wasn't enough for you. You had to make sure we all died here too!"

"John."

"Shut up!" he said interrupting me while pacing. "I know where they are."

I rose up from my slouched position with hope.

"Where?"

"About six or seven hours west of here, I ran across it while I was following you, but I couldn't catch up to you because you ran all night like an idiot."

"Is it very big?"

"Yeah," he responded, "I couldn't get close, but it's big, real big. They live in caves... hundreds of them in the side of a mountain, but if I can get this bomb in one of the bottom ones, I think it will do the trick."

"Then there is hope!" I said happily. "Just point me in the right direction and then you can get the hell out of here."

He came over to me and jerked my collar, ignoring my wounds and got so close our noses touched.

"Listen to me," he said gritting his teeth, "you are going to do exactly what I say. If you don't, I will kill you."

I could tell from his demeanor that he meant every word.

"As long as our bomb cooperates, I should be able to make it there in about six hours and if you head back in the opposite direction toward the compound that should give you about a twelve hour head start. That ought to be enough, but you better not stop for anything, not even a piss," he said contemplating.

"John," I asked pleading, "let me do it."

"Don't argue with me on this one Alex," he said exasperated. "We don't have time for it."

"I know, give me one more chance," I begged again.

"This is our last chance!" he said placing the bomb back in my pack and putting it over his shoulder. "This damn thing could touch off at any moment, so start humping it."

"Cynthia... I mean think of her."

The mentioning of her name infuriated him and he instinctively threw a short punch. I raised my hands up in defense, but they did little to slow its force and his fist struck me in the jaw, sending me to the ground in a daze.

"Don't you try and use her to win this argument. I am a soldier and this has to be done," he told me, "and I am going to make sure it is done right."

"I don't want you to die John," I said to him with a lump in my throat. "I feel responsible."

He walked over to me, kneeled down and put his hand on my shoulder.

"All is forgotten between us friend," he said. "What I said earlier was in anger. You are the only one who is still holding your mistakes against you."

Tears began to form in my eyes and I felt an admiration for John that I had never felt for another person. Not being much for emotion, he ignored my reaction and began walking toward his objective. I knew he would not fail, as it wasn't in his nature. I did as he said and with nothing but my pistol belt and gun began my hike back toward our compound, stopping as John spoke to me for the last time.

"Tell her I love her," he said pausing for a moment before jogging out of sight into the forest.

I watched him disappear forever before running back toward the compound. I ran as often as my condition would allow and walked quickly when it would not, all the time waiting and dreading what would soon come to pass. One hour after another passed with no explosion and I began to wonder if I had gotten too far away to actually hear it or if it would happen at all.

The blast was so sudden that it was over before I realized what had happened. The ground below me vibrated for just a moment then reestablished itself in silence. A few more moments passed and then a sound much like that of a flashbulb going off reached me. I knew it was over and that he had somehow succeeded. I fell to my knees and cried, for a hero and friend.

The trip home was a long cheerless one, for I had little desire to return back and tell everyone of John's fate. Each step I took was both slower and smaller than the one before until I was eventually shuffling along like a monotonous zombie. It was as if my internal battery had given out. If a band of Chassers had run up on me I wouldn't even have given them a struggle. It had nothing to do with my wounds and all to do with my loss of heart.

When I made the compound, my condition was near death and I collapsed into Edmund's arms, not caring if I lived or died. When I awoke I found myself bandaged in the infirmary. Edmund was sleeping in a chair in the corner. After a few minutes he opened his eyes and awoke from his slumber as if he had sensed my consciousness.

"Once again, Dr. Berman has snatched you from death's doorstep."

"How long have I been out?" I asked him groggily.

"You have been under for nearly a week."

"I assume everyone knows what happened?"

"Yes," he said sighing, "the whole lot of us being scientists, made our assumptions and have dealt with it the best we can. I think having you as a patient has been the only thing that has kept Cynthia rational."

"Did it get them all?" I asked referring to the bomb.

"Our satellite feed showed quite an explosion, but we're not completely sure at the moment."

Not knowing what to say, I leaned back and closed my eyes.

"What now?" I asked him.

"As soon as you are able, we are moving," he said. "Everything is packed and ready to roll."

"Move," I asked him, "to where?"

"To a valley between some mountains west of here," he said, "the very spot that Dr. Kineard had originally chosen. With us not being completely sure if the blast eliminated the threat of the Chassers and what effect the fallout may have…we thought it would be best to relocate."

"Site A," I responded. "Even after his death, he still manages to be right."

It was only a matter of a few days before I was well enough to travel. Just about everything from our compound had been disassembled and loaded onto heavy machinery. It had to be one of the oddest looking conveys the universe had ever seen. It was slow going, but for once we had time working for us. Edmund and Jenna appeared to be in good spirits considering our recent past. Edmund would stop our convoy and jump off his tractor upon sight of any new species of plant. Understandably, Cynthia remained distant from us and we left her alone to grieve John in peace. I could tell from her gestures that she was still having difficulty in accepting his absence. I realize now, with everything put into perspective, that he was a good man, something that my personality conflict with him in the beginning kept me from acknowledging. The loss of a loved one, especially a life mate, is something that a person has to work through in three steps: mourning, acceptance and finally continuation. The only partner to such a loss was time, for it does heal all.

Our trip to Dr. Kineard's site A would take us nearly three months, time we desperately needed. I returned to my writings and chronicled every detail of our journey revealing everything, including our successes and failures, without omission. I wanted every fracture we had suffered to mend and I believe that acceptance can only be achieved through the truth.

Through assisting Edmund, I became an amateur botanist and developed a love of the soil and the life it helped to both create and sustain. Edmund led us well and after three months we reached our destination. The four of us stood in the cool shadow of the range and gazed at its magnificence. They were as tall as any mountains I had ever seen in the universe and actually ran nearly half the surface of Hipparchus II. Being our last hope, we named the entire mountain chain the Mountains of Hope and named the mountain we finally built our settlement on Kineard's Mountain to pay respect to the father of our expedition.

In the next few weeks, we rebuilt our compound and although its accommodations were modest in comparison to our first we held more pride in it than in anything we had done before. In my work, I compared our genesis team to that of the religious story, the Garden of Eden. Even in a perfect environment, much like Adam and Eve, we fell from grace through our own deficiencies. What had started out as a beautiful dream, ended up becoming a nightmare of murder and deceit. It seemed no matter how civilized man became deep inside him were the savage roots of his past, ready to overtake him at any moment.

Although I never saw Hummer again, I had a feeling that he survived the blast. We had saved his life and in return, he had done the same for me by warning me that fateful night. As I continued with my work, I couldn't help but contemplate my place in the universe. The very decision I had made to exalt my work would more than likely bury it from the eyes of man and for once I would live my life for now, instead of for my work tomorrow. I always believed it was my disappointment in man that led me to pursue a career in alien psychology instead of the traditional field of human psychology, but after studying the Aluta and the Chasser, whose violent tendencies were on opposite ends of the spectrum, and seeing the flaws in their societies, I came to the conclusion that man held a type of chaotic balance. We came from the universe, a chaotic and turbulent system. Maybe harmony was never intended.

Although I continued to study and write about alien psychology, I undertook a far greater task and began what I hoped would be my final work: *Studies in Alien Nature, Volume Three twenty one, Homo sapiens.*

After we completed our compound, we sat and watched both the suns of Hipparchus II slowly fade beyond the Mountains of Hope. Edmund sat holding Jenna and Cynthia gently reached out and held my hand. I don't think at that moment in the fading dusk, it had any deep significance, except forgiveness and possibly, a new beginning.

# The End

# Suspended Hell

## Private Coller

# Cosmic Contemplations

P rivate Coller cursed quietly to himself as he finished attaching his external armor to his BDUs. His squad had already wasted six and a half weeks traveling across the desolate space that separated Space Star Four from the cold dead planet of Parthuam. He had never even heard of the damn place until he had read its name in their orders the night before they left the comfort of their base. Its coordinates were well beyond those of the Milaone Zone, which everyone knew was the limit of the United Galactic Systems' legal obligation to protect its citizens, as well as its jurisdiction. As the law had been since its first creation thousands of years ago, it applied only to those without political clout or money. If this handful of miners had been anybody besides prospectors for the rich and powerful mining corporation, Glemcon, Coller and his squad would still be back in the warmth of their barracks.

"I wonder how much money the U.G.S. is going to rake in for this little operation?" asked Private Murawski sarcastically.

"I don't know," replied Private Raimom in a similar tone of disgust, "but I guarantee we won't see any of it."

"Will you two stop bitchin'?" yelled Corporal Ellison in a thick Deurum accent. "Hell, if I had wanted to hear all this complaining, I would have brought my wife and her sister. At least that way I might have gotten laid."

"Yeah, but by which one?" replied Private Coller sniggering.

"Hey, I don't need any of your shit either," said Corporal Ellison with a little smile. "Let's just find these fuckers so we can go home, but to answer your question, my wife doesn't put out."

"That's not what I heard," said Private Murawski.

Several of the men laughed.

Corporal Ellison raised his hand as if to smack him, but playfully said, "Why I oughtta!"

Private Coller knew that the corporal was right. All the complaining in the universe wasn't going to reverse orders directly from the U.G.S.

"You boys better strap in," said a voice over the intercom system, "we are about to make entry."

Sergeant Williams came down the hall that led from the cockpit, took position next to Corporal Ellison, and strapped in with the rest of his platoon. After putting on his helmet and sealing it, he spoke through the suit's internal intercom system.

"Now..." said the scratchy voice of the sergeant pouring into Private Coller's helmet, "the computer says that the atmosphere we are about to enter is safe, but I want everyone to stay in level five until I say otherwise."

Their tiny ship began to shake violently as they entered the chaotic outer atmosphere of Parthuam and Private Coller could hardly hear the sergeant's voice that continued to transmit inside his helmet.

"Remember," it said again, "this planet has never been officially explored or properly secured, so be ready for anything."

Private Coller spent the next five minutes praying that their ship wouldn't break apart while he held onto the straps of his seat. He had always hated intergalactic landings more than anything else he had experienced in the marines, primarily because he was helpless. He felt like a sardine being shaken in a can. After several more moments of rattling, a loud thud surrounded the men, followed by a long hiss from the landing gear and then silence. The five men sat buckled in the dull red light of their ship's interior until the pilot's voice transmitted into their helmet's intercom system.

"Sergeant, everything is clear for your departure, but we appeared to have landed just below an electrical storm." The voice paused for a second and then continued in a genuine tone of concern. "Good luck."

"All right everybody," said the sergeant, "you heard the man. We're not here for a vacation. Unbuckle and move out."

A long hiss once again filled their small compartment as the back door slowly opened and lowered to the planet's surface. All five men stood in awe as the image of Parthuam's surface appeared from behind the door. The ground was black as coal and covered by a chalky black dust. The sky above rumbled with thick black clouds as dark as night, swirling in a violent rage. Long red streaks of electricity jumped from the clouds, making long cracking noises that pierced what otherwise would have been dead silence. After several long moments of observation, Sergeant Williams motioned for his men to step outside. Above, the sky danced with ferocity, but the air below was strangely quiet and eerily still. It gave Private Coller a weird sensation, as if they were standing in the eye of some massive storm that would eventually catch up and tear them and their little ship into shreds.

"Murawski," said the sergeant's voice, "what are the atmospheric readings?"

Private Murawski pulled out a small hand held monitor and after a few seconds took an atmospheric reading.

"All readings are green," he reported.

"All right Raimom," commanded the sergeant, "dress down to level four."

Private Coller could see the look of fear in the eyes of Private Raimom after hearing the dreadful command. No one, not even the man that gave the command liked to hear it. It was the last command that many marines ever heard. Raimom was the lowest ranking of the squad and by marine code was required to be the first to unmask and check the safety of the surrounding atmosphere. Although their sensors said the atmosphere was nontoxic, only an actual test would suffice. He hesitantly pulled back his helmet and took a short breath before closing it again. The five men waited quietly to see if he had inhaled any strange toxins. Private Coller could only guess what Private Raimom was feeling and wondered if he would have been as brave. Ever since he had been trained in atmospheric testing, he had always had a fear of being the first to test the air on a strange and unknown planet. After several minutes, Corporal Ellison, hooked up Private Raimom's suit to his M2 monitor and gave a report.

"All vitals are normal," he reported with a sigh.

A full salute of smiles took hold of their five man squad and the second command of atmospheric testing from Sergeant Williams was greeted with little concern. Private Raimom pulled back his helmet one last time and began to breathe normally. After several minutes passed and several normal M2 readings, the squad was ordered to the comfort of level four.

Their mission was to find a small crew of Glemcon miners that had been sent here nearly six months ago to prospect the lonely and unknown planet. The marine's landing coordinates should have been exactly that of the lost mining expedition. Fortunately, all Glemcon employees, much like space marines, were required to have tracking chips surgically inserted into the backs of their necks upon contract into their profession. Their transmissions had ended almost immediately after their arrival on Parthuam. Glemcon reported that the planet's chaotic atmosphere must have interfered with their broadcast in some way. The question that Private Coller had was why hadn't the miner's returned? Maybe the electrical storms had disabled their ship during landing he thought, comforting his mind.

"Victor wun," said the sergeant into his internal microphone using strict military transmission protocol, "this is Victor too. Can you read me over?"

"Roger Victor too," responded the voice from the ship," I am sending you the ship's main tracking signal… out."

Each man pulled down a small slender bar from the side of his helmet and waited for the transmission. A small blue map projected from lights on the sides of their helmets broadcasting a signal from the lost ship onto the tiny screens.

"There she is," said the sergeant looking at the red dots on his transmission screen. "Let's get this over with so we can get off this planet and back to base."

After a few more commands, Raimom took point and they began their march through the black dry soil of Parthuam. Private Coller wasn't familiar with the mining profession or signs of a good prospect, but this planet appeared to be rich in mineral deposits. Its hard surface crumbled away with each step and its constant cloud cover smothered out any possible rays of light from its nearest star, leaving its hard, black, chalky soil free of any visible vegetation, ideal for mining extraction. Now he understood why Glemcon was so interested in this distant hunk of rock. With no life forms to impose mining penalties, the company would be able to completely strip the planet of its natural resources over time with immense profit. He might as well be standing on a planet of gold.

The terrain ahead was wide open except for a few small hills connected by short spurs that ran along the west side of the formation. Occasional red sparks from the chaotic sky above helped light the men's way across a vast black desert. Private Coller still had the same uncomfortable feeling that he had felt when they were first exposed to the strange planet's atmosphere. Everything just seemed to be too calm… too quiet.

"Sergeant," cried the voice of Private Raimom over the air, "I have made visual contact with the landing pod!"

"Hold your position," replied Sergeant Williams motioning for his squad to move ahead. "We're on our way."

The four remaining men ran up the black chalky hill toward Private Raimom's location. They found him in a prone position, staring off into the distance through his laser bics. Taking a cue from Private Raimom, Private Coller knelt down beside him and peered through his laser bics in the same direction. The ship was an unimpressive sight covered in rust and dents with numerous oddly shaped external robotics most likely used for collecting samples and performing other tenuous mining labors.

"No signs of movement," reported Private Raimom.

"Maybe they are all dead," replied Private Murawski.

"Who gives a shit?" said Private Raimom excited. "Alive or dead, either way our mission is over. All we have to do is find them!"

"Will you two shut up? If you were trapped here would you be sitting out in the open getting a tan?" yelled Corporal Ellison.

"Coller, Murawski, get down there pronto and secure the ship," ordered the sergeant. "This mission is not complete until that ship is secured and every one of its crew members are accounted for."

Private Coller and Murawski straightened up their gear and slowly walked toward the quiet little mining ship that rested just below the black ridge formation where their platoon stood. Private Coller pondered if anything could possibly live on such a dead planet. They had failed to see any signs of vegetation or moisture, yet the gases that filled its atmosphere, as well as its temperature, were analogous to that of other planets where life forms were abundant. Either way, he thought, all they had to do was find the lost miners and return home. His ponderings would eventually be solved by the scientists who would examine every inch of this planet, once the U.G.S. had engulfed it into their ever-growing Milaone Zone, a doctrine that protected its citizens and their assets.

With no terrain features to obstruct the two soldiers, they reached the small rusty ship in short order and began their inspection.

The two men made a quick outer inspection of the ship and after finding nothing unusual reported back to their waiting platoon.

"Everything appears to be normal," reported Private Murawski.

"Coller," said the voice of their sergeant, "move in and sweep it out. If a friendly was in there he should have already made contact with you when you came into his sensor range. Be careful."

Private Coller cautiously walked over to the ship's main hatch and tried to open it. Surprisingly, it wasn't locked and swung open with a long moaning creak, letting the black dust of Parthuam that had collected around its seals fall into the darkness of the ship's interior. The hatch on top of the ship was adequate for a normal man, but for a space marine in level four battle dress, it was a tight fit. Coller gave Murawski a long concerned look before following the order of his sergeant. His armor scraped the side of the hatch as he crawled through and dropped to the floor below. He quickly gathered himself and turned on his night vision goggles. A deep green tinted world appeared before his eyes and once they adjusted, he could see as well as he could in broad daylight. The interior of the ship was crammed so full of mining equipment that there was barely enough room for him to move, let alone search it. But in a matter of minutes he had explored its entire interior, finding nothing out of the ordinary. It appeared to have been simply abandoned.

After reporting the area clear, Private Coller crawled out and sat down next to the miner ship to await the arrival of the rest of his squad. They had already completed half of their mission and he sat speculating if it wasn't the most important part to Glemcon. What did they really want? A galactic size company like Glemcon didn't care about a handful of lost miners or the loss of such a tiny old ship, at least not enough to spend as much money and pull as many strings as they did to get his squad here. Besides, why didn't they just send another ship to find out their status? It had to be something more. It just didn't make any sense. Within moments, the rest of the squad made visual contact.

"Victor wun…" reported the sergeant, "we have found and secured the ship, but no signs of the crew, over."

"Roger victor too," replied the stale voice from their landing ship, "sending you their personal ID transmissions, over."

A flurry of small red dots appeared on their visors' monitors, representing the signals from the lost miners' personal transmission chips.

"They all appear to be clustered together," replied Private Murawski.

A long high-pitched whining, as if something was gearing up, startled the men of the squad and Corporal Ellison nearly knocked himself out jerking up his rifle. The head of Private Raimom popped up from a hatch in the ship.

"The ship is functional, it just cut its own power to conserve energy," he reported.

"Great," said Corporal Ellison aggravated, "now get down here and quit playing around! Do you remember anybody telling you to get in that damn thing and start pushing buttons? God damn, it's like I brought my kid along."

Private Coller and Murawski both tried to hold back their laughter, but failed miserably.

"Alright let's finish this," said the sergeant in a determined tone that had been the trademark of space marine sergeants since their first creation. "Raimom, take point again and stay in front of us making sure everything is clear. Murawski, how far?"

"I'm getting a reading of only a few hundred meters?" he replied in a questioning manner as if his readings were too good to be true.

It was difficult for the men to believe that the crew was so close, especially since there didn't appear to be any real terrain features to cover so many men.

"Well, let's quit standing around here like idiots," said the sergeant signaling for Private Murawski to follow the transmission.

With Private Raimom off in the distance, the remaining four men followed Private Murawski like lost puppies.

"Only a couple of hundred meters now," he said in a monotone while observing his visor's monitor.

After a few more minutes he stopped and began to look around.

"What's wrong Private?" asked Corporal Ellison.

"According to my readings, they should be somewhere around here."

Sergeant Williams ordered the men to disperse and police the area.

"I don't understand it," said Private Murawski, slapping the side of his GR sensor in frustration.

"Let me see that," said Corporal Ellison. "He's right. It's almost as if we are standing on top of them."

Everyone froze and stopped what they were doing before looking down at their feet. After staring at the ground blankly, Sergeant Williams looked up at his squad with dismay.

"You don't mean we are going to go down after them, do you?" asked Private Murawski apprehensively.

"Our orders are to return them, dead or alive," said the sergeant apathetically.

"No fuckin way I am going down there!" screamed Private Raimom pointing toward the ground. "I mean we don't even know how the fuck they got down there!"

"There has to be some type of passage," said the sergeant almost to himself, "some kind of cave or hole."

"You can't be serious!" screamed Private Raimom in a childlike pout.

"Aren't you getting tired of me telling you to shut up?" screamed Corporal Ellison at the top of his lungs.

"Yes!" screamed back the private.

"Then shut your fucking hole!" replied the corporal.

"Alright, let's police the entire area around this spot," commanded the sergeant. "They didn't just pop down there."

The five men began to search the vast black desert of Parthuam in hopes of finding some kind of clue to the lost crews' whereabouts. After several moments without success, a cry came across their intercom system.

"You guys better get over here!" it said. "You are not going to believe this!"

After getting a location, the rest of the platoon scrambled and found Private Murawski peering off the top of a hill. When Private Coller reached its edge, he stood mesmerized. It was an astounding sight unlike any he or any other marine had ever seen. Stretching out from their ledge was a large flat valley of black sand and in its center stood a tall black plateau with an enormous opening in its face. What made it so unusual was that an immense prodigious light emitted from its core lighting up the black valley, as would a sun a universe. All along the valley floor were little purple plants that seemed to thrive in the light that radiated from the strange cave opening. It was a bizarre sight especially standing under the red energy riddled black sky of Parthuam. Private Coller's hair stood on end as if he was about to be struck by lightning.

"What the hell is that?" asked Corporal Ellison.

"Is it man made?" asked Private Murawski.

"I don't know, but I think we found out how they got below us," said Sergeant Williams despondently.

"I knew this mission was going to suck!" said the expressive Private Raimom.

"You think every mission is going to suck," responded Corporal Ellison.

"Victor wun," said the sergeant reporting back, "do you read me, over."

"Roger victor too," responded the voice on their intercom system, "loud and clear, over."

"We have encountered a strange light phenomenon and are going to check it out, over."

"Roger," replied the voice again, "keep us updated on your position and report back every hour on the hour, out."

"Alright, let's try and get this over with and get out of this weird place," said the sergeant looking around. "Something about it doesn't settle right with me."

The five soldiers began the long descent into the valley below and reached its flat surface with little difficultly. Private Coller didn't care for the dry chalky surface beneath his boots, but somehow the great light secretion engulfing his squad had a serene calming beauty to it. To be under such a violent storm and yet find everything completely still, including the fine loose sand at their feet was abnormal. As the spread formation of men marched closer to the great white light, Private Coller tinted his visor to help his eyes adjust.

"Strange," said the sergeant using his arm to cover his eyes, "that light doesn't seem to be radiating heat."

It did seem kind of unusual to Private Coller that something so bright didn't emit even the slightest hint of warmth. He looked up toward the bright pulsating light, but its intensity forced him to look away just as he noticed a long black object floating across the sky.

"Get down!" he screamed.

The men dropped to their bellies and rolled into defensive positions. They tracked the object with their sights and waited for the sergeant's command to fire. The unidentified black object slowly made it way toward their position until they could see that it was a creature, nearly three feet in length that looked something like an insect with long dual quad wings. The thing slowly hovered past the squad without giving them a moment's attention and flew into the mouth of the cave, disappearing into the giant light.

"Okay," said Private Raimom nervously, "now I know I'm not going in there."

"What the hell was that?" asked the corporal, missing an opportunity to order Private Raimom to shut up.

"I don't know, but it didn't seem to be very concerned about us," replied the sergeant.

"That's what got those stupid miners!" screamed Private Raimom. "The hell if it's going to get me!"

"If you don't shut the fuck up we are going to make you go in there and introduce yourself to it!" screamed the corporal, not missing another opportunity to shut up his whining private.

"We at least need to call for back up!" replied the almost hysterical private.

"Where the hell do you see any back up?" asked the corporal in a belittling tone while stretching out his arms. "What are the two pilots on the ship going to come down here and do your job?"

"Calm down," said the sergeant in a soothing voice. "What we saw is simply an alien life form that hasn't given us any reason to consider it an actual threat."

"So what you're saying is that these bugs and the miners we are looking for are good friends and they are in there having coffee together?" said Private Raimom in a sarcastic tone.

"Hey watch your tongue private!" yelled Corporal Ellison.

"Either way," replied the sergeant, "we have to get those men out."

"I'm with Raimom on this one. Maybe we should wait for some help," said Private Coller.

"Do you want to wait six weeks in this hell hole for another squad to arrive?" asked the corporal.

"It doesn't matter," replied the sergeant calmly. "This is not a democracy and we haven't encountered anything here to warrant another squad or platoon to be dispatched. So loosen up your panties and buckle up your helmets because we are going in."

At the command of their sergeant, the men went back to combat level five, which consisted of their regular armored BDUs and a clear, tough exoskeleton helmet that completely covered their heads. As they continued toward the light, the walk on foot become more difficult as the terrain began to elevate toward the cave. They struggled to keep their footing in the loose black soil and eventually had to holster their rifles so they could use all their limbs to keep balance. As the walk became a climb, Private Coller took second in line behind private Raimom and after several tedious moments they made a small precipice, which lead up to the cave's large sixty plus feet opening. The light coming from it was so bright that none of the men could look directly at it, forcing all of the soldiers to stare down at the ground.

"Raimom..." said the sergeant before being interrupted by Private Murawski.

"Something is all over my suit and mask," he said in a calm monotone.

Private Coller looked up from the ground and under the searing illumination watched as a shiny silk-like substance engulfed Private Murawski. He tried to go over and inspect his comrade, but stopped when he discovered that his suit was covered in tight silk as well. Private Murawski began to scream in agony. The scream came through Private Coller's helmet at a deafening tone and sent him into a panic. He began to tear at the constricting sticky substance that seemed to be trying to overcome him by sheer weight. More screams entered his helmet's intercom system as well as the seeping sounds of short quick heat lasers being fired in defense. Not knowing where their enemy was coming from, Corporal Ellison began to fire randomly into the bright light that beamed upon them. Murawski, trying to break free of his bonds, stumbled and fell into Private Coller, gripping his arms so as not to fall. Instinctively, Coller reached up to grab hold of his cohort and break his fall. The action dislodged his rifle from his shoulder dropping it onto the ground. Murawski's helmet clashed up against his own and for a moment they looked into each other's eyes. Private Coller could see the fear of the unknown in

123

his comrade's eyes as he was torn from his grip and jerked up into the air, disappearing into the bright light above. The force of his friend being jerked upward pulled him forward causing him to fall face first onto the ground. The strange film that covered him spread over more and more of his body as he lay flat on the ground, so much that he could feel its weight beginning to hold him down.

Trying to raise himself up, he could see Corporal Ellison still blindly firing his rifle into the air hoping to hit whatever was spraying the men with the constraining web like substance that now covered the corporal's entire body. Watching the corporal, Private Coller reached over and grabbed his own rifle to give himself a small amount of security, when a large black creature nearly twice the size of a normal man with bright red markings lowered itself above the frantically firing corporal and gripped him with its numerous long black scaly legs. Their sharp points pierced the corporal's tough exterior armor and tore into his soft flesh, causing the screams of fear that had filled Private Coller's helmet to change to those of agonizing pain.

Seeing a friend and fellow soldier torn apart rattled Private Coller and all thoughts of helping his platoon were obliterated by the aura of fear that took hold of his consciousness. His only thoughts were of escaping the sudden horror that had befallen his squad. Pulling his heat knife free from his belt, he began to cut away at the silver strands that were restricting his movements. His knife carved them away easily, but as he cut, more began to pour onto him, slowly covering his face shield and trapping him in darkness. A new isolation came over him as he was enshrouded within the darkness of his own suit. This time, a more intense panic overcame him and he went into a claustrophobic paroxysm, tearing and cutting at himself in a blind rage. He screamed in pain as his own heat knife tore into his flesh as he frantically tried to cut himself free from bondage. In a sudden jolt, his legs came up from the ground hoisting him into the air like a bullet. The sudden jerk of his lift dislocated his legs and caused him to lose his grip on his heat knife. He began to spiral into the air upside-down as if he were on a sadistic amusement ride. The blood in his body flowed violently into his head, making Private Coller feel as if his skull was going to explode from the pressure of intercellular fluid within his neurons. His eyes bulged behind his eyelids as his temporal artery swelled and pulsated furiously. He frantically continued to tear at his bonds with the rage of a caged animal. Then suddenly, his ascension stopped as his body entered into a strange limbo. The last thing he could recall was swirling his arms as he plummeted into a freefall.

When Private Coller regained consciousness, he found himself covered in a heap of hardened silk. His tough clear helmet had shattered from the fall and the only thing that separated him from the environment of Parthuam were the strands of silk that covered the facing of his helmet. He tore the thick durable fiber from his face and found himself in some type of underground chasm. His body was covered in dried blood from self-inflicted wounds and upon trying to stand up he found that one of his legs was broken. With closer inspection, it appeared that the long strands attached to his legs had been torn in his frenzied cutting and he had tumbled down into some hole below the great light. His legs ached around the sockets in his pelvis and on his first attempt to stand up he collapsed. After falling a second time, he painfully slid his body backwards using his hands and leaned against the wall. His movement caused loose pieces of chirp to break free and stir up a fine dust that made him cough and wheeze uncontrollably.

"Is anyone out there?" he asked in a cough through his squad's internal intercom system.

Nothing but an eerie dull radio silence responded.

"Hello," he screamed into it, afraid of being alone, "please somebody has to be there!"

His hands began to shake uncontrollably upon finding himself isolated. He paged back to his ship in a near panic.

"Victor wun," he paused for a moment, "this is Victor too. Can you read me over?"

Silence and isolation began to close in on him feeding on his consciousness flowing over him like water.

"Victor wun," he screamed again, "we are in need of back up! I repeat we are in need of back up!"

He began to scramble through his belt and found that he had lost both his rifle and heat knife during the earlier attack and cursed to himself silently. The hole was dark, with just enough light from the strange source above for his eyes to adjust. As he began to assess his surroundings, he noticed through the falling dust that the hole wasn't a hole at all. Rather it was either the beginning or the end of a long narrow crevasse. Once again he scrambled through his belt and although he had dropped both his rifle and heat knife during the scuffle, his flashlight was still attached. A bright concentrated beam leaped forward from Private Coller's small handheld flashlight, piercing the darkness. While fanning the dusty air to ease his breathing, he managed to get himself up onto his one good leg for a better look around. He could see the ledge that the strange light sat on above, but it was nearly forty feet straight up. It would be nearly impossible for a man in top physical shape to scale, yet alone a man in full combat gear with a broken leg. He began to hobble down the long crevasse, examining its walls for a suitable spot to climb out. Dust boiled up into the dry air as he dragged himself along, until it was impossible to see more than a few feet. Before he knew what had happened, he stumbled over a small indention in the crevasse floor and fell face down inside the opening of a large cavern. The thought of what might lie ahead in the darkness caused him to quickly push himself up from his helpless position and slide himself back out the way he came in. Regaining his composure, he realized that what he had discovered could have been far worse, such as a long steep dead end. Besides, the crevasse behind would be a certain death trap if he happened to be spotted by one of those horrible things.

Using his flashlight, he nervously shined it into the deep darkness hoping not to illuminate one of the creatures or reveal his location. Although his flashlight emitted a sharp concentrated beam of light, the darkness and dust before him hungrily swallowed it as if he were peering into the mouth of a black hole. Once again, he pulled himself up to his feet and with the support of the crevasse's wall, began to slowly make his way deeper into the cavern's mouth. For several feet the light struck only black air and swirling dirt, then his eye caught a sparkle ahead. With each step he took, the sparkle grew larger until it morphed into a brilliant motionless lake that was as smooth as glass. Not a ripple formed upon it has he slowly examined it. It was immense and extended as far as his light could expose in the vast darkness ahead. He began to limp toward the strange lake, when his eye caught another sparkle within the pool. Two distinct round marbles of gold stared at him from the murk of the pool. Every muscle, organ and tissue within his body froze! They were eyes! Dozens gazed at him intently from within the quiet pool. To what unfathomable beast did those eyes belong? It was chilling to Private

Coller to even speculate on a creature that could dwell in an inky pond below the surface of such a distant and unknown planet. After seeing how easily the spider like creatures had dispatched of his squad, he feared what else this strange planet might have to offer to a lost and wounded man.

Having little recourse and lots of curiosity, he continued his slow shamble toward the still eyes watching him intently to see to what they belonged. With every step his light revealed more of the objects within the gel until before him laid the ashen beholder of those eyes. It was the blood covered and distorted face of his squad sergeant! The man's face was a ghastly pale and void of life with glowing unblinking eyes that penetrated into Private Coller's soul. He continued to scan the pool and discovered the bodies of Ellison, Murawski, Raimom, several of the miners they had been sent to find and various other creatures, unlike anything he had ever seen, of all shapes and sizes, including one that looked exactly like the flying being that had passed them on their way to the strange light. It was a grizzly sight to find a pool that was nothing more than a transparent graveyard. How pitiful the bodies looked trapped in death as if on exhibit.

He gently reached down and touched the surface of the pool and found it was not a liquid, but more of a thick gel-like substance. It actually set around his finger, held it there and settled down to a polished glassy look. His finger escaped its grip with ease and within seconds it was as if he had never touched it at all. The bodies within it were in some type of suspension. His heavy legs easily tore through the colloidal solution as he limped out to retrieve his sergeant. Although the sergeant's armored body was heavy, Private Coller had little difficultly dragging it back to the shore as the sergeant's body glided smoothly across the lake's gel surface. Once he sat down on shore, the pool looked as if it had never been touched, as the sergeant's body lay limp and covered in its excretion. He carefully cleared off his sergeant's face, out of respect, and left him to go retrieve the others. He began to wade out toward Corporal Ellison's body when something startled him.

"Private," said a lifeless voice.

Private Coller swung around, making a sucking noise, as his legs broke the pool's hold. He squinted in the darkness from which the sound came finding nothing, but the motionless body of his sergeant.

"Sergeant?" asked the private unbelievingly.

"Come," said the moving lips of Sergeant Williams.

In an almost boyish excitement, Private Coller ran over to his sergeant and gripped the man's head in his hands. He wasn't alone! Thank God, he wasn't alone anymore, he thought.

"Oh my god," replied the private in an elated voice, "you're alive!"

"No," said the struggling voice, "I'm not alive. I've just been preserved from death. Those damn things paralyzed my body. I can see, hear and speak, but I can't move or feel anything. I am in some sort of conscious death!"

"Don't worry sergeant," said Private Coller in a reassuring tone, "as soon as I get the rest of the squad out, I'll get us out of here somehow."

"No!" said the sergeant choking. "It's too late for us. You have got to get back to the ship and warn the others not to come looking for us. I don't want another soul to live in this type of suspended hell."

"I can't leave you here, marines never leave anyone behind," retorted the private.

The sergeant's eyes stared into his not having blinked once the entire time they spoke. "God no!" cried the voice. "You won't be leaving us alive! My pistol should still be in my holster... take it."

Private Coller rummaged through Sergeant Williams' BDUs and found his pistol. He gripped it in his hand and showed it proudly to its owner. A long moment of silence passed between the two men with the dead eyes of the sergeant staring at Private Coller. He knew what the sergeant wanted.

"I won't do it!" cried the private.

"Listen," said the sergeant, "I am giving you a direct order. I want you to shoot each one of us in the head and then return to the ship. Then, they can come back with a company and blow the shit out this cursed light and its keepers."

"Sergeant," yelled the private in tears, "I can't do it! I tell you! I can't do it! It would be murder."

"Please son, I want this more than anything I have ever wanted. I am in some unnatural state between life and death. Those things are using that light to attract prey like some kind of ancient bug trap and that shit you found me in is nothing more than a preservative," pleaded the sergeant. "Those things drink our blood! I can feel them as they drain my life from me and just before my heart stops and I am almost free of this hell, it stops! The damn things won't let us die! I just want it to be over. I want this nightmare to finally end."

Private Coller took the pistol and placed its tip squarely into Sergeant Williams' forehead and wavered.

"It is okay," said the motionless body in his hands. "I am already dead."

The blast was quick and did little more than stop the motion of the sergeant's lips, for his body was as it had been, lifeless. Quickly, before the horrible beast above could come below and put him into a similar semi-death state, he waded out into the gelled pool and put each man of his platoon and every miner he could find to rest. Being a true soldier, Corporal Ellison was still holding onto his rifle with a death grip. By taking hold of the large weapon and placing his sergeant's pistol in his belt, Private Coller felt safer knowing at least with such weapons, the hideous creatures would never take him alive.

Fearful that something might have heard his pistol blasts, he began to look for a way out of the strange graveyard. The pool seemed to go on endlessly, but further out, in the walls above its surface, were holes emitting the strange bright light from above. Once again, he hastily rushed into the gel pool and waded out toward one of holes. The further he went the deeper the suspension became until it was up to his waist. He stepped around one poor soul of a creature after another that had been lured to its doom by the strange light on his way to what he hoped would lead to freedom. He began to fear that he might not be tall enough to reach the closest hole, when the pool floor leveled out.

He was nearly at the first hole, when a dark object came into sight. He stood completely still lowering his chin to the surface of the pool, barely breathing so as not to disturb its glassy plane. It was one of the spider like creatures! It had a large pudgy body that was covered in long black hair and bright red markings. It slowly glided across the pool with its eight crab like legs searching for a late night snack. It didn't appear to notice his presence as it carelessly glided along the surface of the lake, as if it were on ice. Along its way, it used a long hose like orifice from its face to check on its captives by draining blood from their bodies. It would shrewdly suck blood to satisfy its hunger, mindful not to kill the captive. Then after making horrible sucking sounds, it would move on and repeat the exact same process with each victim it passed. Not wanting to confront the repulsive creature, Private Coller began to slowly move toward the wall.

A shriek that nearly tore out Private Coller's eardrums came from the beast as it spotted his movement. It began to skate toward him at lightning speed swinging the long hose like orifice from its face in wild stimulation. The first shot Private Coller fired from his rifle tore off several of its legs on its right side, disabling it and stopping its advance. The second shot hit it directly in the body spinning it onto its back, where it slowly sunk with a long sucking sound beneath the surface of the suspended lake to spend eternity with its captives.

Afraid of the attention his last two blasts might receive, he quickly maneuvered toward the wall and used his hands to drag his body through the deep murk of the lake and reach the first opening. The hole opened into a long slender tunnel shooting almost straight up. He managed to scale it after several failed attempts and eventually made the ledge above the great light and the area where they were first attacked. The light, although not giving off any heat, was so intense that he couldn't bear to look at it directly. He made his way to the ledge stopping at a mortifying sight.

Beneath the ledge hanging from long strands were dozens of the black beasts, haunting the strange light for prey. He swiftly stepped back and lay down on the ledge. If one of the creatures spotted him, he wouldn't stand a chance. He gripped the handle of the pistol in his belt. If he were to fail, there wouldn't be anyone to save him as he had saved the others. He would have to do it himself or face the possibility of spending eons in a suspended hell. Then, with celerity of a man bursting with adrenaline, he jumped up onto his good leg and began firing at the misshapen monsters hanging on the walls below. His first shot hit one directly in its fat body and sent it tumbling down into the crevasse below. Another shot disabled one's two hind legs, forcing it to shoot a long webbed rope out of its tail to save it from falling. The remaining creatures began to shriek madly and swarm his position.

## Suspended Hell

He fired again hitting one in the face, causing it to tumble into the light. To stay a moving target, he limped along the ledge and continued to shoot at the pursuing beasts. Another fell to his gun, but within moments of his first shot, several had made it onto the ledge with him. Then in a bold attempt to escape, Private Coller went feet first into a sitting slide down the ledge toward the base of the light. Dirt boiled up around him and small rocks that broke loose from his slide bounced up and tore into his hands and face. His attackers began to shoot webs at him in an attempt to entangle him, but his fast slide made him a difficult mark. No matter what happened, he couldn't allow himself to tumble over to where he could be knocked unconscious. Afraid of being captured alive, he leaned back and gripped his pistol tightly so as not to lose it while bouncing toward the light.

At the end of his slide, his broken leg hit hard against the bottom of the ledge fracturing clean and exposing both his tibia and fibula bones through his skin and suit. Ignoring the pain and thinking of nothing but escape, he leaped off the ledge below the bright light and tumbled down to the dark Parthuam desert floor. Trying to get up and run, he fell face forward and after realizing his leg could not hold him anymore, he quickly pulled his pistol free, put it to the temple of his head and rolled over to see how much time he had before he would be engulfed in their fury, but shockingly he found himself alone on the flat desert floor. They had not come after him, but instead ran around the walls of their great light as if they were repairing it!

He had done it, he thought, screaming within his own thoughts. He had escaped hell! He turned onto his belly and lifted himself onto his one good knee and dragged his bad leg toward the landing ship. At one point he saw another one of the long gray insect like creatures fly by and out of mercy he shot it down with his pistol before it could make it to the great light. He did little more than say: "You're welcome" and continued on with his long slow crawl back.

The two pilots, who had come to look for his squad when they had failed to report, found him near the miner's rusty ship and helped him back to the landing ship. After hearing his story, they buckled up and began the long journey back to Space Star Four.

As they broke the atmosphere of Parthuam, Private Coller sighed for the loss of his entire platoon, but couldn't help but think about the odd white light he had seen and its even stranger keepers. How did it gain its strange power and was it merely to attract prey or something much more? It didn't matter now, he thought giving a rough half toned psychotic laugh. When his company returned, it would serve them as little more than an illuminated target and the only ones to profit from it would be Glemcon.

# The End

# The Genetic Game

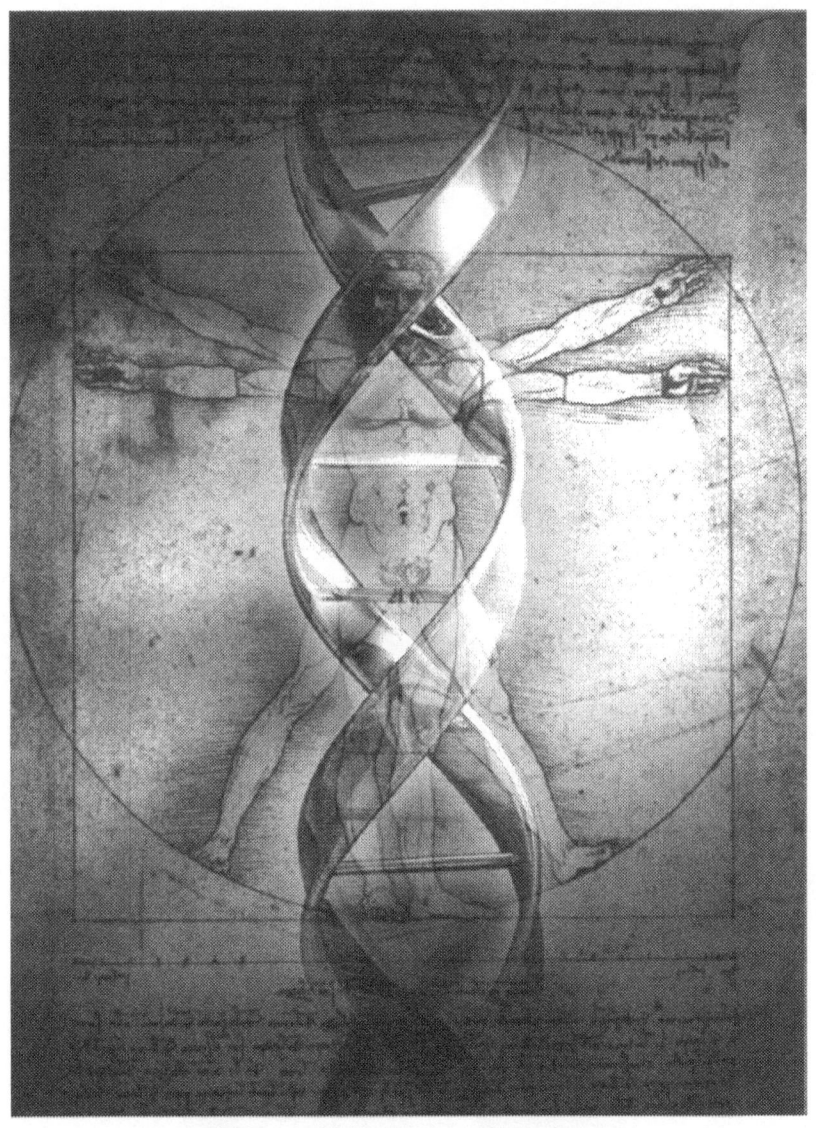

## The Code of Man

# Cosmic Contemplations

# Part I
# Payback

C aptain Armonil's ship sped through space attempting to escape every planet, ship and memory that lay in the wake of the vast cosmos. It was what lay ahead, infinite space that bore some shred of hope. Hope that maybe they could outrun everything they had ever known and be forgotten forever among its incalculable stars and endless systems. What chased the small ship was pure hatred, bent on nothing less than extinction of Captain Armonil and his people. A force determined to erase them forever, not only as individuals, but also as a species. Although Captain Armonil had spent his life as a chef and his ship had been built as a cargo vessel to transport grain across great distances of space, years of service while on the run had changed the two into hardened battle veterans. His men followed every order and accomplished his commands with unwavering resolve, not only because he demanded it, but also because they were part of a system where failure could mean their demise.

Captain Armonil had been the master chef of the Roué, a world renowned restaurant in France, when the extinction of mankind began. What was thought to be a huge meteor shower harmlessly passing near the Earth was actually a cloak for an invasion force unlike any known to man. Thousands of ships swooped into the Earth's atmosphere from behind its cover and began to lay waste to Earth and its occupants. At the time, the men of Earth had colonized numerous planets across the universe, but had never encountered another form of intelligent life and therefore were not only surprised, but also dreadfully unprepared. The phikogars, as the few men that escaped would later come to know them, were a fanatical and deeply religious species that believed they had been chosen to eradicate the universe of all other inferior life. They zealously slaughtered every man, woman and child they encountered in the name of their fierce and demanding god, Giouaal. Their vehemence made no distinction whether their enemies were peaceful or not, as all suffered the same horrible fate. Centuries of hunting down and destroying life across the universe had rendered them ruthless and efficient exterminators. Only those that took to ships and fled into the depths of space survived the initial attack upon Earth. Tens of thousands of ships of various types and sizes made the rush into space. Only half survived the onslaught laid upon them by the phikogar fighters that were sent in pursuit.

It was rumored that a few men did not take to space and survived the first invasion of Earth by going underground to resist their invaders. Later, Captain Armonil had heard through transmissions that the use of a bomb with properties similar to that of a bug bomb had poisoned the Earth's atmosphere, leaving not a man, woman, child or creature alive on its surface.

Once man had been eliminated from Earth, the phikogar began to search out and destroy every other planetary settlement they could locate. What happened next was what had hardened Captain Armonil, his crew and their altered ship the *Barley Belly*. Every ship that had broken through the phikogar armada had been pinpointed, counted, tagged and assigned a stalker ship by the phikogar race. These stalker ships were specifically built to hunt down and destroy runaway ships or what the phikogar's called genetic capsules. If one ship survived, the phikogar would fail the will of their mighty and unforgiving god, something that no living phikogar had ever done. Once a stalker was assigned a ship, it would never receive another order until its mission was complete. The *Barley Belly*'s stalker had been chasing them for over five years.

Captain Armonil's crew initially consisted of one hundred and twenty six men, eighty seven women and fourteen children, all having a crucial role in their survival. Each man, woman and child was a member of one of three separate, but equally important casts: officer, soldier and worker. Captain Armonil ran his ship much like he ran his kitchen. Everyone had a specific set of duties and everyone was well trained in their position. No one questioned his authority, for he had saved them all in the beginning and it was he that kept them alive today.

"Captain," said the ship's master, "our scanners have picked up a small vessel orbiting the surface of the planet ahead."

"Bring us in underneath it," he ordered. "If it's a live ship, I want to be on it before it has a chance to spot us."

"Yes sir."

"Set a 45 degree course for 3 full segs, then set a 90 degree for one half a seg," ordered the captain.

The master's mate took heed of the commands and set their course precisely as he was told.

The men in the bridge stood quietly as they closed in on the unknown vessel, then suddenly the master's mate pulled off his voice-com and yelled to the captain in his own voice. "It is a phikogar scout!"

The captain took to his chair and began firing commands.

"Do a full force docking on it now!" he barked. "Do not attempt to destroy it unless it leaves orbit."

The officers surrounding the captain began to swarm around the bridge, preparing to implement a hostile docking on the enemy ship just identified. The *Barley Belly's* bow, which had been initially built with a large round docking door to dock with other trade ships, had been modified by its men with dozens of small lasers spaced around the exterior of its docking door so that it could quickly burn small holes just millimeters apart, making a small detonation entry easy once it attached its seal to another ship's hull.

"Captain," said the ship's master, "first platoon is at the docking door ready to deploy."

"Good," replied the captain. "Mr. Duchey, you are in charge of the bridge. I am going to get me some phik."

The captain rose from his chair and put on his pistol belt. The rest of the bridge recognized the change of command and proceeded with their duties. The captain quickly left the bridge and made his way to the prow of the ship, where he found a squad of soldiers standing ready.

"First sergeant," screamed the captain.

A short stocky man in a soldier's uniform came up and stood at attention in front of the captain.

"Captain," said the first sergeant, "first platoon is good to go."

"I want this done right sergeant. No fuck ups...no transmissions, no escapes, no mercy," ordered the captain.

"Yes sir," said the first sergeant.

The first sergeant turned around and addressed his handful of men, twenty to be exact, four squads of five men. "Men you heard the captain. We don't get many opportunities to strike back at the fuckers that destroyed our homeland. Make it count!"

"Yeah!" yelled the men of the first platoon in unity.

Eagerness overcame the waiting men, an eagerness to give payback to those who had ruined their past and threatened their future. Sweat began to bead upon the tense men of the first platoon, as they stood ready to engage the enemy. The captain felt the same emotions as his men. His teeth gritted in anticipation. He wanted to feel his knife sink into the flesh of another phikogar. A long creak filled the air, followed by the loud thud of a collision. After attaching to its target, the *Barley Belly's* docking door opened and made its cut. Two men from first platoon quickly ran up to the exposed side of the enemy's ship, set two small charges and stepped back. A quick flash and dull explosion blew the weakened wall inward, exposing the ship's interior. The men of the first platoon ran in screaming, ready to kill anything that appeared to hold some form of life. The captain went in with his men and engaged the enemy. They had taken the small vessel by surprise and within a matter of a few minutes the boarding action was over leaving the small enemy ship and its crew at their mercy.

"Captain," yelled a young soldier with pride, "we have taken one alive!"

The captain followed the soldier and found a phikogar wounded and trapped by a beam that had fallen on him during the docking's explosion.

"Well if it isn't a sack of phik shit," said the captain speaking directly to the trapped phikogar. Its long gray soft body oozed a clear coagulate that protected its body from both dehydration and contaminates, but to the men of Earth the protective gel appeared to be nothing more than disgusting slime. It stared up at him from its helpless position with the determination of a tarikon warrior.

"You have accomplished nothing," it said slowly raising its long five-jointed finger at the captain.

Its use of the human tongue did not stun the captain, for he had heard them speak before in other encounters and through their transmissions. They were such efficient exterminators, that they had actually studied the Earth and its occupants for years before their invasion upon it, learning its occupant's culture, language, technology and most of all, their weaknesses. Their culture and beliefs allowed no room for failure.

"Oh, I beg to differ," said the captain in good humor. "I accomplished taking your ship and killing everyone on board... except you. How does it feel to be helpless before your conquerors, to fail your god?"

"It feels blessed to know I am going to die in his service," it said slowly. "It is only your horrid stench that makes this moment unpleasant."

The captain kneeled down beside the wounded being and took hold of its neck to shut it up and then looked directly into its large glassy eyes.

"Don't enjoy it too much," he said angrily, "it's not going to last very long I assure you."

He pulled out his knife and forced its point against the phikogar's chest.

"I want you to take a message to your beloved Giouaal," he said. "Tell him I said to send more."

His knife went in the alien's chest and began to make tearing noises as the captain twisted it back and forth inside its flesh. He wanted to cause pain, for causing pain to the phikogars and cooking were the only things that made him happy anymore. He despised the species so much that he could hardly bear to hear the phikogar wheeze as it died and abruptly stood up giving it a quick kick to make its last dying breaths cease.

"Sergeant," yelled the captain full of adrenaline, "check the computers and see what they were up to and if they sent any transmissions. I also want anything on this ship that is edible or of potential use to be moved to our ship. We needed to be out of here ten minutes ago."

"Sir, do you want us to scuttle the ship?" asked the first sergeant.

"No," he replied, "chop off their heads and shoot them into orbit. I want the phikogars to find the bodies here and their heads orbiting the planet."

After calming down a bit in his quarters, the captain returned to the bridge.

"Sir," reported the ship's master, "Corporal Enisen from first platoon is hailing us."

"Put him on," ordered the captain, still tense from his last kill.

A voice filled the room, "Sir, the phikogar scout ship made a transmission to its mother ship before we boarded it."

"Get all of our men off that ship now soldier," ordered the captain. "We need to put as much space as we can between here and nowhere before that transmission reaches its destination."

"Um," said the broken voice, "it didn't report us. It reported a human settlement on the surface."

# Part II
# Snatched from the Grip of Death

The bridge of the *Barley Belly* erupted into commotion from both disbelief and excitement as its men struggled to comprehend what such an unexpected report meant. "People way out here?" said an officer.

"How did they get all the way out here?" said another in bewilderment.

The captain's mind began to wonder, he had spent the last five years doing nothing but running and making token strike backs at the enemy that did little but appease his own hatred and anguish for a short time. Now he had the chance to do something meaningful once again. They could steal the fate of these people from grip of the phikogars.

"Mr. Duchey, get those coordinates and prepare to land," said the captain.

"Sir," said the ship's master, "we could travel through space for five more years on the amount of fuel we will consume landing and returning to space."

"Mr. Duchey," replied the captain calmly, "do you think those people below give a shit how far we could travel on the fuel saved by passing on their rescue? Do you realize how much food I would have saved if I hadn't brought you all with me? The next time I want you to question one of my orders, I will ask your opinion on it. I will not stand around and let a phikogar kill another human being if I can help it."

"Sorry sir, I didn't mean to offend," he replied quickly.

"No offense taken Mr. Duchey, just complete your duties."

"Yes sir!" replied the ship's master.

The scorned officer thought nothing else of the incident and continued with his assigned task without animosity toward his captain. He had stepped out of line and had merely been corrected, that was all. Not a single man, woman or child on the *Barley Belly* would contemplate the matter any further. Once the officer fulfilled his required duty, it would be as if the incident had never happened. That was how life was among the residents of the *Barley Belly*. Everyone aboard the ship scrambled to his or her positions once an announcement was made indicating the captain's intention of landing the ship. Excitement ran amuck the ship's inhabitants as no one had set foot on the surface of a planet for nearly five years. A few of the younger children who had been born on the Barley Belly had never stepped foot off of it. Their only image of the outside world came from the few books aboard the ship and the bedtime stories told to them by their parents.

Although solidly put together, the *Barley Belly* shook and rattled severely during entry into the planet's thick atmosphere and for a brief minute the captain began to wonder if she would hold together. She held true and the crew cheered as the ship settled down into a smooth flight path.

"Sir," reported the ship's master, "we have made visual contact with the settlement."

The captain stood up, leaned over his pilot's shoulder and stared through the tiny window in front of him. Large smoke stacks rose high into the sky, bellowing ebony smoke into the air. The buildings themselves were of a simple but efficient dome design, similar to those of Earth's first distant settlements' structures. If the captain's historical knowledge was accurate, many of the early deep space settlements and their colonists had lost contact with Earth and were never heard from again. Maybe he and his crew had inadvertently discovered one such settlement he thought. It was the only explanation that made sense. All the other known settlements from Earth had been attacked simultaneously with the invasion and all were warned through distress signals upon the destruction of Earth. The ones who survived were the ones that used ships, as had the captain to escape into the vast universes of the endless cosmos.

"Make a direct pass over them, but go slowly so not to alarm them," ordered the captain. "Then make a landing in that valley at nine o clock."

The large freight ship sailed gently over the quaint settlement and bore left landing softly in a lush valley near a large lake. The people of the small settlement stopped their daily tasks, transfixed upon the passing craft, for this settlement was over one hundred and eighty years old and not a single living soul in it had ever seen a functioning ship. The *Barely Belly's* gut opened wide giving birth to the ship's captain, its first mate, and the twenty men of first platoon, spawning the men into the bright open sunlight. Their pupils swelled nearly shut having adapted to years under the dull artificial light of their ship's dark innards. A large party of men and women, nearly three times the size of their landing crew, met them half way between their landing point and the town with smiling faces.

One of the men in first platoon whispered to his friend, "They have black women," he said in excitement, for he had not seen a black person since he had left Earth and men currently outnumbered the women of their ship by eighteen.

Two cultures, as different as night and day, stood eye to eye, one with dark ebony glistening skin formed under the strong suns of Eudaemonia and the other pale and pasty white from the shadows of an enclosed ship.

"Welcome to Eudaemonia," announced an older woman with swaying silver hair, "I am Felicity, the eldest of my people."

"I am sorry to bypass formality," said the captain firmly interrupting her, "but unfortunately we do not have time for small talk. Every second we waste here significantly reduces our chances for survival."

"Time spent is never a waste," she said calmly, "it is only time unspent that is lost."

"You must amass your people without delay, I doubt we have more than a day or two before a phikogar stalker or frigate arrives and obliterates this settlement," said the captain, ignoring her philosophy.

"What is a phikogar?" asked the elder woman unfamiliar with the term.

"A vile race of beings that plans to destroy everything within sight of your settlement, including your people, if you are unfortunate enough to still be here when they arrive."

"The wars of men are of no concern to us. It was for such things that our foremothers brought us here, so we could live in peace. We are a peaceful people, why not a woman, man or child has raised a hand in violence in Eudaemonia for three generations."

"That is of no importance to these bastards. The only thing that concerns these beasts is that you are breathing."

"Please, you and your people, come with us, we can eat and discuss these matters further on comfortable rugs with full stomachs and reasonable minds."

"I am telling you for the last time, there is no time for such things! At this very moment phikogarian ships are barreling toward this planet with one purpose... the extinction of the human race!"

"I assure you, we have no intention of leaving our home, and if these phikogars come, then we shall reason with them as I am reasoning with you."

The captain stepped back in frustration, rubbing the sweat from his face with the palm of his profusely callused hand. He had not felt the heat of the sun against his pale skin in nearly half a decade. He pulled out a small communicator and called back to the ship's bridge.

"Mr. Bryne, get second platoon out here with loaders ASAP!"

"Yes sir," replied the master's mate, "right away!"

"Mr. Duchey, have the men of first platoon gather every man, woman and child and put them onboard the ship. As soon as second platoon arrives, have them load everything worthwhile onto the Barley. That means anything edible... I want livestock and anything that might be used as fuel on our ship before we leave."

"Sir, what if they resist?" asked the ship's master.

"Did I give you any options in that last order?"

"No sir!"

"I want us back into space within six hours, not one minute later."

"Yes sir!"

"This is preposterous! The things you are talking about are not yours. You cannot take us against our will!"

"Trust me, you will thank me later."

Following the orders of their first sergeant, the soldiers of first platoon began to round up what had been a welcoming committee, despite their obvious disapproval.

"We will do no such thing! This is the Promised Land, the utopia that man has strived to recreate since the Garden of Eden... please it is for everyone. You and all of your people are welcome to share in our blessings here," said the eldest women pleading with the captain.

"This place is going to get ugly real quick once the phikogars arrive. They are going to turn your little Garden of Eden into the pits of hell," said the captain.

"No one here is going to raise a hand to assist you in your war. War is the highest of sins, a weight upon the soul that can never be lifted from an eudaemonian."

"This is not a war we are involved in, this is genetic cleansing! Do you know what a phikogar does to its victims? It burns them down slowly to a fine ash to completely eliminate their genetic code and they will not quit until every human being, including their DNA is extinct, conscientious objector or not."

"I do not believe that any living creature could harbor such raw abhorrence toward another living creature. The scripture teaches that all beings possess the ability to love, if only shown love first."

"This would be much easier on all of us if you would just cooperate. Will anyone of you help us?" he asked screaming over the eudaemonian leader. "Everyone of you are coming, I need someone to make sure we don't leave anybody or anything behind."

"No one is going to help you forcibly remove us from our home!"

Before she finished her sentence, a young man hesitantly stepped out of the crowd. The wise elder noticed his movement from the corner of her eye and spun around to challenge him with words, for violence to her was not an option.

"Heinrich, what do you think you are doing? Step back before these men condemn you with their violence."

The captain saw his opportunity and seized it by shielding the boy from his authority figure with a quick step in between the two so not to force the young man to challenge her instructions. The captain hated to undercut her authority, especially as a leader, but he knew what would happen to these people if they were left behind.

"Young man, I am Captain Armonil, I need you to go with Mr. Duchey and help him salvage anything that might be of use to us. It is very important that we don't leave a single piece of food or livestock behind, but no luxuries are to be brought aboard." He seized the boy's two shoulders and looked directly into his eyes, to pass on the importance of his mission. "For God's sake do not let us leave anyone behind."

The young man felt the magnitude of his words and followed Mr. Duchey and his men as they wrestled with the reluctant group of eudaemonians. He liked the captain and his men. He had never seen men of youth in positions of leadership. In his culture the oldest woman of the tribe was always its leader, passing on leadership after death to the next oldest member. Only women were allowed to be elders, since they were less inclined to violence and were therefore believed to be more rational. It was the written word and he had never doubted its validity, until he saw that a man could hold a position of power. A soldier stepped up to sequester the tribe's elder, only to step back from her defiant stance.

"Young man…" she stated with the clout of a mother scorning her son, "don't you dare lay a hand on me!"

The captain stepped up toward the spirited old woman, picking her light frame up into his arms as if she were just a child.

"Unhand me!" she screamed.

"If I don't are you going to strike me?" he asked curiously.

"Of course not, as a eudaemonian I have forever denounced violence."

"Good, that's going to make things easier," he stated carrying her with her flinging arms and legs back to his ship.

The men from first and second platoon stripped the picturesque settlement, loading everything of value into their great ship's belly, leaving behind a lonesome scene of fading smoke stacks burning in the wake of their escape. Although the world they left behind was one of calm serenity, life aboard the *Barley Belly* turned into that of chaos as two divergent cultures clashed.

The captain sat in his quarters alone studying the many files of the phikogar scout ship they had raided earlier in the day searching for clues, anything that he could use against his mortal enemies. He wanted so badly to quit running and take the fight to the phikogars, had it not been for his people, he would have quit running a long time ago and ended the miserable existence of constant flight, taking as many of his pursuers with him as he could manage. A knock at the door broke his concentration.

"Come in," he grumbled.

The door opened revealing the face of the ship's master. A flood of arguing echoed in from the halls, disappearing as he slammed the door.

"Sir, the men of the ship are complaining that the eudaemonians are distracting them from their work."

"Hmm... I know the feeling," he said looking back down at his computer screen. "If they touch one of the men, haul them off to the brig. If not, then ignore them."

"Sir, they are not physically stopping the men from working, they are standing in the way and screaming at the top of their lungs to harass them."

"Are they babies? Having to work under such conditions is good training. Tell them I expect them to be able to do their jobs under any circumstance."

"Yes sir," said the ship's master with a helpless look.

He opened the door, letting in the sounds of screams, only to seal them off again as he left. The captain returned to his frustrating search through the many files on the screen in front of him, only to be interrupted by another knock at the door.

"Come in," he screamed in aggravation.

The sergeant of first platoon stuck his head into the small room.

"Sir, Felicity would like to see you."

"Get in here and stand at attention, just because the rest of the ship has gone bananas doesn't mean you can poke in here like a damned civilian."

"Yes sir, sorry sir," he said standing at attention. "Felicity would like to speak with you."

"What does she want sergeant?" he asked annoyed.

"Sir, she is asking for her people to be returned to their planet immediately."

"You knocked on my door to tell me that? You think I don't know that is what she wants?"

"Sir, permission to speak freely?" he asked.

"Permission granted."

"I knocked on your door sir because she won't go away. She has been nagging me like a second wife for nearly an hour. I am about to crack her skull. I have to hear that crap every night when I go back to my quarters. I can't stand it all day too!"

"Send her in," he said brusquely.

"Thank you sir," said the sergeant grateful to have rid himself of the ornery old woman who had been badgering him since they had entered space.

Within moments, a gritty woman with long swirling gray hair and an unwavering face stormed into his quarters, bound and determined to gain back the freedom of her people.

"How dare you not even have the dignity to speak to me after kidnapping my people and plundering what has taken us nearly two hundred years to construct."

"It is far too late for any debate," said the captain calmly staring at the enraged woman. "Even if you pummeled me in a debate and I agreed that everything you said was correct, I still couldn't take you back. To do so would be suicide for both of our people."

"The time for reason was when we first met," she screamed with a red face and enlarged veins in her neck, "but you refused to listen to me then and now you say it is too late! Do you always twist everything in your favor?"

"The reason I didn't listen to you was because you know nothing of the phikogar and therefore you couldn't possibly understand the magnitude of the situation."

"I am not a child that you can bully around! I demand you return our people to Eudaemonia right now!"

"I've already told you there is no way we can go anywhere near that planet," he said in exasperation of having to repeat himself to the woman. "It is probably already infested with those slimy bastards."

"Then I demand you set us down on another inhabitable planet! We want no part of your war!"

"Calm down for just a moment, my officers and I are having a dinner celebration tonight and you and your elders, as I believe you call them, are invited. We can talk more then."

"And I assume this invitation is similar to your last one in that I have no choice?"

"You don't have to come, but since your people and my people have to get along on this tub, it would be nice if we, as leaders, led by example."

"To lay a hand on any living creature with the intention of harm means eternal damnation to a eudaemonian, but knocking that smug grin off your face would almost be worth it!" she screamed, before stomping out of the room and slamming the door.

"Wonder if that was a yes or a no?" said the captain lightly to himself before continuing on with his research.

# Cosmic Contemplations

# Part III
# Cultures Collide

The people of the *Barley Belly* stirred in excitement, as they awaited the dinner fête. There had not been so much cause for celebration in a long time. In just one day, they had overtaken and destroyed a phikogar scout ship, recorded six phikogar kills, restocked their dwindling supplies and saved one hundred and thirty two people from certain demise. It had been the best day they could remember since their days on Earth and everyone but the eudaemonians were ready to celebrate. There would be two separate dinners, one for the captain, his officers and the eudaemonian elders and one for the soldiers, workers and the remainder of the eudaemonians. The food would be the same in both halls, all prepared for this special occasion by the captain, only separate as the captain never let himself or any of his officers fraternize with the soldiers or workers of the ship, unless they were family. The captain and his officers sat down to dinner and after waiting for the elders in vain, the men said a small prayer and began to eat.

"You really outdid yourself this time Pierre," commented the ship's master chewing.

"Thank you Jaques, I still have a few old tricks up my sleeve," replied the captain casually.

The men sat around the table in their civilian clothes, chatting happily, using each other's first names casually, a luxury afforded to them only during dinner. It had been a tradition on the ship since it first launched on its journey without a destination. The captain felt it allowed his men to bond outside of their work relationship. He believed a captain was nothing without a dedicated crew.

"It actually melts in your mouth!" commented the ship's engineering officer. "You have to enlighten us on your recipe."

"Trust me it tastes better if you do not know."

The men burst into laughter, not allowing the sly suggestion to damper their hearty appetites. That task would be left to the stern faces of the eudaemonian elders that interrupted the jovial dinner. The six elderly women had come into the dining hall in single file with austere postures and cold disapproving stares. The captain instantly rose courteously to his feet followed by the other man in the room.

"Welcome ladies, please join us," said the captain, gesturing toward six empty chairs.

"Now we warrant respect?" commented the eldest of the elders, sitting down with two untrusting eyes directed at the ship's captain.

The captain ignored the icy glares and stood up to serve his guest, as would a waiter. Although the captain of the ship, he was still a chef at heart and was not above serving what he had meticulously prepared. Seeing someone enjoy a meal cooked by his own hand gave him one of the few feelings of satisfaction he had known since leaving Earth. Unfortunately, the women he served were not of the disposition, after being ripped from their planet, to appreciate his culinary talents.

"You expect us to sit down and celebrate the kidnapping of an entire culture?"

"We are celebrating your rescue," he rebutted. "I understand your frustration and I am sorry we didn't have the time to appropriately discuss with you why we had to do what we did. So please, rest your mind and hearts just for tonight and appreciate the fine food before you. Tomorrow, I will take the time to show each one of you the ship's records, which have recorded everything that has transpired between man and phikogar since the invasion."

Felicity, the eldest pushed her plate forward curling her nose in disgust, "I will not eat such slop on the worst day of my people's history!"

The five other elders followed her example and all pushed their meals toward the center of the table. Every person in the room, not of eudaemonian descent, froze like picturesque statues, some actually holding their food in mid air with their mouths wide open upon hearing the word slop. No one had ever insulted the captain's cooking before, as he was a gastronomic genius cooking up absolute masterpieces from the skimpiest of ingredients, but primarily because they all respected him for what he had done for them, working tirelessly, eighteen hours a day to keep them one step ahead of the phikogars. The captain's pale white face turned dark red from pulsating blood through the bulging blood vessels in his neck with fire in his eyes. Two sources of anger swelled within his muscles, first being the insult of his culinary efforts and the second being the ingratitude for his acts as a savior. His biceps femoris tightened as he stood up, throwing his chair onto the floor, shattering the silent room with a loud boom. He stood motionless for a moment, at the head of the table, without saying a word. After checking his initial rage, the color in his face faded as he took on the composure of a leader once again.

"Have you ever heard the old saying, when life hands you a lemon, then make lemonade? Well, not ever having set foot on Earth, you might not even know what a lemon is, but right now you are sitting in a big bucket of lemonade. We have made the best out of the absolute worst and because of that, all of your people are still alive. Sure, it may not be the life you are accustomed to, but we all have had to make sacrifices to exist!"

Felicity stood up quickly, throwing her white hair in a whirl of anger that contrasted with her dark ebony skin, ready to match the fury of her male counterpart.

"You did not have the right to take us without our consent!"

"You are arguing about something without all the facts. I, as well as every member of this ship, know damn well, from personal experience, what the phikogars would have done to you and your people. And not one of us could bear to think of such an atrocity after narrowly escaping one in our own world. We did what we did out of love for mankind!"

"We demand that you release all of our people now!"

"And how do you expect me to do that, launch you into space?"

"I expect you to set us down on the next inhabitable planet so we can start anew as did our foremothers nearly two hundred years ago!"

"Tomorrow morning you and I will discuss this thoroughly and if we cannot come to some sort of agreement, then we will discuss your departure. Now please sit down and at least try your dinner before you insult it."

The six women stood up almost in unison.

"This will be the last time I will allow you to delay my people's freedom! I will speak with you in the morning," said their leader leaving the room.

The rest of the eudaemonians followed her lead, slamming the door as they left, leaving the captain and his officers in silence. The captain and his men finished their dinner, saying little else before retiring to their quarters.

The next morning, Captain Armonil awoke to his alarm after six hours of sleep. It was all he would allow himself for he had so many tasks to manage on a daily basis he rarely got to them all. He would sleep even less if he thought it would not wear on him in the long haul. He had lost so much in this struggle and he intended on seeing it through. Failure was not an option. He had given up too much to save his people. He had given up his own wife and two daughters to make the escape into space and although he knew he had to leave when he did and that to go back for them meant certain death to them all, it still wore heavy upon him. As long as he and his people were alive, his family would not have died in vain. A knock at his door startled him as he studied his chart of the stars upon which he had diagramed their course from Earth. Everything had its markings, planets, battles and now, a rescue.

"Come in," he said quickly, rolling it up.

In poked the head of Christophe, his lead engineer, "Sir, Felicity would like to see you."

From behind him came a muffled but distinct voice arguing with the near helpless man, "I demand to see him now, get out of my way!"

Felicity stomped into his quarters as angry as she was when she had stormed out of the dining hall the night before.

"Did you rest well?" asked the captain.

"No, this thing rattles and it's as if there is never a day in this horrible place."

"Please sit down. I have some records I would like you to look over about our history with the phikogars."

"Who wrote them?" she asked smartly.

"Why me," he stated palpably.

"Don't you think it might be biased?"

"If you look at it from someone who is running for their life, maybe."

"Let me ask you something captain," she said sitting across from him with cold piercing eyes. "Have you ever killed or ordered the killing of one of these phikogars?"

"Yes," he said unashamed.

"Then what makes you any better than they?" she asked.

"If someone started killing everyone you know and then tried to kill you, what would you do?"

"By doing so, she or he has condemned their own soul, it would be better to die innocent than to live in damnation."

"I am sorry but the phikogars do not think that way… they believe that there is one great god of the universe, Ontopiuag. They also believe that he is sick and slowly dying and that his final request was that his twelve sons and their creations should fight until only one remains. Once this is complete, he will die and the one remaining son and his followers will live in harmony for eons. Based upon this belief, they have set out on a zealous mission to find and destroy the followers of the eleven other sons. According to their records, they have found and completely destroyed seven intelligent races… we are number eight. It is their belief that they, the followers of the youngest son Giouaal, have became locked in a death struggle with us, who they believe are the followers of the eldest son Jonkierdeat, with no other recourse but extinction for the loser."

"Captain, violence begets violence and if you fight back you will only be met with more violence. Your only hope is to try and reason with them. Surely you cannot expect to run from them in this old ship forever. What type of future is that for your people?"

The captain opened up his mouth to speak, only to be interrupted by a page from the bridge.

"*Captain,*" said the scratchy voice from a speaker in his room, "*We have received an open transmission from Baertuhjk!*"

There wasn't a name in the universe that he hated more. It was the name of the commanding phikogar of the stalker assigned to their ship that had been chasing him and his people for over five years.

"I'll be right there, hold reception until I arrive," he ordered. "Come with me if you would like to meet one of your precious phikogars."

The captain stood ready, in front of a huge blacked transmission screen, with his officers and Felicity at his side. By order of the captain, the clear transmission was received and appeared in front of the large bridge, showing the face and torso of their pursuer. The appearance of its horrible slender gray body and wide intense yellow eyes startled Felicity so that she nearly gasped, but being a strong woman, she quickly regained her composure. The captain stood ready, with a proud smile, he knew why they were receiving a transmission. The phikogar had found the remains of the scout ship that he and his men had raided. The beasts never made a transmission unless they were angry and that alone made him happy, whenever he was fortunate enough to receive one.

"Your little insignificant strike has done nothing more than help us discover your current flight pattern and those that you took with you are only going to suffer your fate," it stated in perfect human tongue.

"They fought bravely, begging only for a few minutes before we killed them."

"Lies!" it screamed in a death shattering tone. "No phikogar has ever begged anyone!"

"Hey, I was there, not you. We actually recorded it for laughs. Would you like to see it?" said the captain, playfully bluffing.

"All of you will pay for this, once we catch you, I assure you that you and your people will suffer as long as possible before I burn you."

"Come on, you have been promising that shit for over five years now. How does it feel to be a failure, before Giouaal?" said the captain purposely to get a rise out of his counterpart.

He had studied their religion for the past five years from captured records, even obtaining a digital copy of their holy book, Kneail, and he knew how to push their buttons.

"Shut up!" it screamed in wild passion, for it was forbidden for any infidel to ever mention their god's name. "You are not worthy of even knowing his name, yet alone to speak it!"

"Who's the infidel here, you or us? Their deaths are on your hands, for had you done your job and captured us, they would still be alive."

"Far more humans have died than phikogars. Your people do not even have a home planet. You're failure is inevitable, it is only a matter of time."

"Ah, that is where you are wrong," said the captain as if having a revelation. "You need to reread the Kneail. The great one is near death and if by the time of his death no son has eliminated the others, then he will die without a true heir and time will stop. Everyone loses."

The strange eerie beast swelled furiously at his mentioning their holy tome. "We know you are running low on fuel, you cannot run forever. Your fate and your father's fate have been sealed."

"Long live Jonkierdeat," said the captain, before signaling his officers to cut transmission so he would get the last word.

"You are the most horrible person I have ever met!" said Felicity shocked by what she saw transpire between the two leaders. "You purposely tried to make things worse."

"It couldn't get any worse unless they actually found us."

"Yes, but it could get better if you tried to negotiate."

"Lieutenant, change course by six degrees west," ordered the captain, ignoring the woman's argument.

"We will not be a part of this war! My people and I want out!"

"If that is what you want, then that is what you are going to get!" he yelled. "Ensign Jaques plot a course to somewhere I can drop this bitch off!"

"Um… yes sir," said the ship's master, unsure how to address the fuming captain.

"Once we find a planet, I will drop you off with the trash. Now get out of my face!"

Felicity stormed out of the bridge, no one had ever affected her the way the captain did. He actually spun thoughts of violence in her mind, which was a mortal sin to her. She had to get away from him and his people while she still had a soul.

# Cosmic Contemplations

# Part IV
# Mutiny

The next morning the captain awoke to the sound of his door opening. His eyelid cracked open slightly, catching several dark shadows pouring into the obscurity of his room. Alarmed, he leaped to his feet, as several bodies crashed into his own knocking him backwards onto his bed. He struggled with a throng of glossy black arms and hands trying to subdue him. He caught one of the dark forms with a sharp uppercut under the chin, sending it back onto the hard floor where the form landed with a deep thud. Rope began to appear from the many hands, entangling his limbs tightly until he was unable to resist anymore. Suddenly, a light came on exposing his mutineers' ebony skin, to be that of the desperate citizens of Eudaemonia.

"Untie me at this moment!" he demanded.

"I am sorry it had to come to this," said Felicity, stepping into the room. "I agonized about this decision all night, but you left me no choice."

"Felicity, let me loose right now! Before I have all of you imprisoned for mutiny!"

"Captain, your jails are full at the moment with your men. This is no longer your ship. I know what we are doing is wrong, but at least no one was harmed."

"What do you expect to get out of this? None of you know how to run this ship and I swear to you none of my people will help you. Untie me and I will let you go free as we agreed earlier."

"We don't have to know how to run it, captain I have done what you have not been able to do."

"What are you talking about?" he asked queerly.

"I have spoken rationally to the phikogars," she stated proudly, "as I tried to reason with you earlier and they have agreed to a peaceful solution to this war."

"What?" he screamed in disbelief. "How did you speak with them?"

"After we took over the bridge, we received another transmission and I negotiated a cease fire."

"Did you close the transmission?" he asked in panic.

"Well no," she said quickly, "they asked me not to, so stay in contact."

"They are tracking it and on their way here right now!" he screamed madly.

"Calm down, everything is going to be alright, I negotiated the freedom of your people. They will be taken back to Eudaemonia with my people to live peacefully. The only stipulation was that you and your officers were to be turned over for crimes committed against their kind, but he assured me you would all receive a fair trial. I am sorry, it was the only way," she said sadly.

"There will be no trial for any of us! As soon as they arrive, they will destroy, you, me... both of our peoples! You must set me free so we can escape, while there is still time!" he pleaded.

"I am sorry captain, but I can't allow my people to play any part in this violence. You had your chance."

"You have doomed us all," he said sadly. "It has all been in vain."

"I am sorry you feel that way captain," she stated, before leaving the room.

She left him tied up and locked in his quarters, with two guards at the door, before going back to the bridge to await the arrival of the phikogars. The captain lay in silence, staring at the ceiling, powerless to save his now ill-fated people and ship. She did not know what she had done, as her heart was in the right place, but that was her mistake, showing heart toward a phikogar. Now they all would die due to man's least known characteristic, compassion. It would be a horrible death. Baertuhjk would make sure of that. He hated mankind with a passion, especially the captain and his men. He would make

160

them all suffer for having to chase after them through the cold infinity of space for five years. The poor children, he thought, oh god, if only it would not have to happen to the children. They would suffer the same horrible fate, more than likely a slow burn, starting at the toes, to erase their genetic material, and then slowly up the body, burning their wounds shut so not to allow the victim to die until the bright flame reached their axial skeleton. The mental thought of such a scene surged adrenaline into his muscles and he struggled to break free with all his might, but the tight bounds only dug deeper into his flesh cutting off the blood flow to his enlarged and failing muscles. He slumped backwards, exhausted from his feeble attempts to break free, in hopeless frustration. If he could have killed himself in that moment he would have done so, not to have to look at another phikogar, not to have to see them win. His door opened once again with a creak, the captain turned his head the best he could to see who it was, but his tight binds held him firmly in place.

"Captain," asked an unfamiliar voice, "are you okay?"

The captain looked over a rope to see the face of the young man who had helped his men against the will of Felicity on Eudaemonia.

"Heinrich! You have got to set me free!"

"Captain, I am sorry about this, Felicity says it is the only way," he said dolefully.

"Heinrich, you are our only hope, if the phikogars get here before we get away, they will murder us all!"

He saw indecision in the young man's eyes. Understanding that this was his last chance, he carefully chose his words to make them count.

"Son, you helped us save your people once, now I ask you to help me save both of our peoples. Felicity does not know what she has done. You need to do this to help her too." The captain paused, watching the young man wrestle within himself, unsure what to do. "Sometimes being a man and a leader means making hard decisions. Hurry in my drawer, I have a knife."

The young man halfheartedly reached over and cut the captain's ties loose with the knife, dropping it to the floor once he was done.

"You did the right thing," the captain reassured the young man. "I just hope we have enough time. Is anyone outside?"

"Yes, two guards."

He took a long look at the cheerless young man, "Do you know how to make a fist?"

"Like this?" he asked, balling up his hand.

"Yes, but leave your thumb out so you don't break it. Then swing it as hard as you can at their face."

They swiftly subdued the inexperienced guards, who as conscientious objectors had never been a fight, and rushed down to the ship's main cargo hold, which had been converted to a makeshift prison a few years ago, in hopes of actually capturing phikogars for study. They had quickly learned phikogars were difficult to take alive and once captured, strangely died within two days of confinement. Using mallets from the kitchen, Heinrich and the captain broke into the prison, overwhelmed the peaceful guards and freed the officers and soldiers. They hastily made it to the bridge and upon finding it locked, tore the door down in a fury to gain access. Felicity and the other five elders screamed in distress at their bold entrance.

"Get them out of here," he ordered his men, while looking at a Heinrich who averted his eyes from those of Felicity's, "but do not harm them in any way. Cut transmission and get this ship moving now!"

The officers of the *Barley Belly* rushed to their posts, put on their headsets and brought life back to their hibernating ship. A long shadow crept across the bridge as a huge ship bore down upon them, engulfing the small vessel.

"Sir it is too late," said the ship's master glumly, "a phikogar frigate has made visual sight."

The phikogar frigate was the flagship of the phikogar fleet. Thirty times the size of their own ship, there was no known craft in the universe that could stand against one. To run now would be fruitless. They would be blasted apart at the slightest movement.

"Has transmission been cut?" asked the captain, astonished by the immense proportions of the vessel.

It stretched beyond the sight of the human eye in all directions, as it had become the horizon.

"Yes sir, I did so as soon as we arrived on the bridge."

"Do we know anything about phikogar frigates?" he asked in awe of the structure hovering above.

"No sir…" said the officer uneasily, "no one has seen one and lived to tell about it."

For the first time since their escape from Earth, fleeing was not an option for the *Barley Belly* and its crew. The only advantage Captain Armonil and his men had over the superior ship besieging their tiny craft was that the phikogars still believed that the ship was in the control of the eudaemonians. If their ship stayed motionless, the *Barley Belly*'s sly captain knew his enemies would board to do their executions firsthand. The more the phikogar made its foes suffer, the greater its personal status would be once Giouaal became father of the universe. The aliens believed this so fervently that they tended to argue like children about who would get to torture their victims to death. They had the captain cornered, but he wasn't out, at least not yet.

"First sergeant," commanded the captain to his top NCO, "I want first platoon, second platoon and any man that can carry a weapon at the docking door now!"

"Yes sir!" screamed the old sergeant, spinning around and double-timing out of the bridge.

"Mr. Duchey and Mr. Rousseau, I want you to dock the ship behind that gun turret. Give us as much time as you can," he said, possibly giving his last order to his two loyal officers.

He turned and stared into the eyes of his remaining officers. Every one stood ready to die by his side. Today they might get that chance.

"Gentlemen," he said to the officers on the bridge, "let's join the men."

They stormed out of the bridge and down into the docking bay of the *Barley Belly*, where they found every remaining male earthling standing ready to fight, along with one male eudaemonian. The captain walked up to the young man and placed his pale hand onto his dark shoulder.

He placed his forehead against the young man's looking into his eyes, "You are one of us now. I am as proud of you as I am of any man in this room."

The large cargo room jerked suddenly, sending the men in all directions as the ship's master fired up the old ship's engines and sped toward the large looming frigate. The small ship's sudden movement startled the frigate's gunners and by the time they started firing, the much smaller vessel was in too close to be targeted. The captain and his men waited anxiously for the connection and explosion that would put them face to face for possibly the last time against their mortal enemies. The small ship attached to the hull of the metal behemoth like an unwanted parasite filling its innards with viruses, in the form of armed men. The hundred plus men erupted through fire and smoke, killing the stunned occupants of the gun turret. Although they had succeeded in surprising their adversaries, they were too few to overwhelm their enemies and their captain knew it. He settled his men down, keeping them under control so they wouldn't run off like maniacs attacking the superior force of phikogars.

"No one moves or says a word until I say so," ordered the captain to his top officer. "Pass it on."

His officers passed the word along as the captain found his top technology officer.

"Dial in and find their bridge," he ordered softly.

The young man pulled out a long wired socket and dialed directly into the ship's computer. They had taken a lesson from their persecutors about understanding your enemy and had figured out the binary code of their computers from previous encounters, something the phikogars did not know about their opponent.

"I've got it!" declared the young man proudly.

The large group slinked through the gigantic ship killing every phikogar squad that was unlucky enough to find their location on their way to the ship's control room. Unable to pinpoint their rapidly directed movements, the phikogars couldn't muster up a large enough force to stop the advance. By the time the phikogars discovered the men's objective, it was too late to stop the men's assault. Ninety seven battle hardened men flooded into the frigate's large control room, slaughtering its occupants in a harsh hand to hand battle that spilled blood from both species. In its wake, seventy two men stood ready for their next objective.

Captain Armonil stood among his men, covered in the blood of both his friends and enemies. The death of his men weighed heavily upon him even in their victory. His men were more than pawns to him they were and always would be his family.

"Tap into the mainframe and shut down every compartment in the ship," he ordered to the technology officer.

The young man plugged a small hand held electronic unit into the huge central computer of the bridge.

"I'm in!"

"Lock down the entire ship. No one moves or leaves until we say so."

"Yes sir."

"How many phikogars are currently onboard?" asked the captain weighing their options.

"The log states a standard frigate crew is sixty two hundred sir," answered the young man hesitantly.

Sixty two hundred was entirely too many for his men to handle with small arms and although his technology officer had deactivated the frigate's weapon systems, the *Barley Belly* designed originally as a freight ship, did not have any gun fittings and therefore could not attack the large vessel. Its destruction would have to come from some other drastic method, maybe through a collision course with some galactic body or self-destruction. The captain knew they didn't have much time before the crew of the giant war frigate would began to advance to the bridge, where he and his men were too few to hold them off for very long.

"We don't have much time. We need something," he said in desperation, "anything we can use to destroy this ship and its crew!"

The phikogars were so confident that their frigates were unbreachable that their computers were without code, a miscalculation that would cost them dearly.

"Sir, we have control of life support," stated the young officer.

The captain's mind churned orders, "Cut life support, and then set the CPU to lock open every portal on this ship in five minutes. That should give us just enough time to make it back to the *Belly* and undock. Once the portals open and we detach, the hole we leave will suck the life out of everything in this oversized tin can. Then we can return, ransack this tub and recycle it into the nearest star."

"Sir," screamed the young officer stumbling upon a new discovery, "there is a bug bomb on board!"

The captain had wondered how such a large ship had beaten Baertuhjk and his ever-persistent stalker to their location. Now it all made sense. The frigate had been dispatched to Eudaemonia with a bug bomb to ensure the death of the entire planet when the phikogars received the final transmission of the small scout ship that his men had destroyed in its orbit. This completely changed his strategy. He had just reclaimed his queen in a chess match of survival, now he would go on the offense.

"Set the timer, time is now of the essence."

"Sir, it has been set!" screamed the young man.

The captain of the *Barley Belly* ordered his men out of the bridge and into the long hallways of the immense frigate. They ran down the halls recklessly trying to reach their ship before the timer opened every door in the ship and unleashed thousands of phikogars. If they got pinned down, they would never make it out alive. The portal to their ship was still intact as the men swarmed inside, closing off the wide docking door with only a minute to spare.

The small ship broke free like a full tick from its prey, escaping the wide looming shadow of the frigate. The captain and his officers ran to the bridge, stood in front of its small window and watched nervously as their plan stood ready to unfold. If their plan somehow failed, the mighty guns of the war frigate would blow them apart, silencing his people forever.

The huge war ship's computer unbolted and opened every door inside its hull, forcing the ship's thick concentrated air to rush out into space through pressure gradient. The men aboard the *Barley Belly* cheered as dead phikogars and debris drifted into the cosmos, crystallizing upon hitting the cold of deep space.

"Mr. Duchey," said the captain, interrupting the premature celebration of his men, "organize every man, woman and child into the main hull... including the eudaemonians. We have matters to discuss."

The ship's master looked at him queerly, but upon seeing the stern face of the captain, he went below to gather up everyone as ordered.

# Part V
# Suicide Run

___

Captain Armonil stood grimly in front of curious eyes, both earthling and eudaemonian as he prepared to give what might be his last speech. He had made a hard decision and for the first time since taking command of the *Barley Belly*, instead of giving orders, on this next mission, he would ask for volunteers.

"I'm not sure if we earned it or if we just stumbled upon it, but today mankind has received a golden opportunity to strike back at those who wish to see us dead," he explained calmly. "Sitting upon that frigate above us is a horrible weapon, capable of destroying an entire world and I intend to return it to its rightful owners."

Everyone held his or her tongue, even the normally vocal Felicity stood silently among her people, in respect of his authority.

"It will be a difficult mission and I can't guarantee success. The only thing I can guarantee is if you volunteer for this mission you will not be coming back," he stated truthfully. "All I need is a large enough crew to crash that frigate onto Tarikon and set off its payload."

Men began to step forward one at a time until every remaining earthman and one eudaemonian stood before him ready to die by his side. Mankind was not a selfish beast with only self-preservation in his or her heart. They could sacrifice for others, they were worth saving and his men had proven it. They were better than the phikogars and he and his men would deliver a blow to even things up in their genetic, winner keeps all game. He stepped forward and began to pick the volunteers he would need, choosing only those that were absolute necessities. He chose his technology officer, because they would need him to manage the ship's CPU, two pilots and all of his officers, sixteen in all, save Mr. Duchey, whom he promoted as the new captain of the *Barley Belly*. Although he did not want the position, he followed his final order from Captain Armonil with the intention of seeing it through as he had all his captain's orders from day one. The young eudaemonian that had saved them all by going against his own fundamental beliefs, confronted the captain in disappointment of being left behind.

"Captain, I mean no disrespect in challenging your decision, but I have been watching your men and I have learned a lot. If you let me go, I promise you, you will not be disappointed!" he pleaded.

"Son, it is because of you that all of us are still here. I have spoken with your new captain and he has agreed with me, you are to become an officer," he replied, offering the *Barley Belly's* highest honor. "You have already done more in the war against the phikogars than all of us combined. We need you here to dissolve the differences between our two peoples."

He rubbed the young man's short curly hair, promoting him from a mere child to a leader of men. Felicity's deep brown eyes locked onto his and for the first time they were soft, without judgment. Although she did not understand the war she found herself and her people in, she did understand the sacrifice he, all of his men and one of her own were so readily willing to make.

It was a short goodbye as the *Barley Belly* quickly re-docked upon the ghost frigate floating aimlessly through space, depositing the captain and his valiant volunteers in environmental suits. Within a few short hours, he and his men sealed up the huge gaping hole left by their forced docking and fired up the ship's life support system. Under command of Captain Duchey, the *Barley Belly* disappeared into the depths of space, leaving a handful of men speeding toward Tarikon, the home planet of the phikogar.

According to the ship's computer, at full speed it would take three months to reach its orbit, whether they would make it or not, the captain was unsure. It wouldn't take the phikogar long to discover that they had lost contact with one of their frigates, once transmissions began to go unanswered. Although he knew the phikogar would begin to search for the lost frigate, he only hoped they wouldn't connect the lost frigate in relation to he and his men and cut them off before they reached the orbit of Tarikon.

If the phikogars found the stolen frigate before they got to Tarikon, there would be little hope of success, as he didn't have enough men to properly maneuver the immense ship or to make an attempt to return fire.

During the three long months of the trip, the men studied the large ship's files and structure learning more than they ever wanted to know about their enemies. Not only did they discover the phikogar fleet's numbers, like how many frigates, stalkers and scout ships were active, they also learned the phikogar's estimate on human beings that remained alive. According to the phikogar's calculations, the number was just over eighteen thousand. It was such a small number thought the captain sadly, but at least they were not alone in the last war of man. He hoped that on this mission he would not let mankind down.

The small group of men ignored phikogar transmissions on a daily basis in hopes of not to encounter an enemy ship on their journey. It was a long quiet trip where he and his men had time to make peace with themselves and their actions. When their ship finally reached the orbit of Tarikon, not a single man on board regretted their decision to come.

What the men didn't know was that nearly a month ago, a small phikogar scout ship had spotted the hijacked ship and reported its location and flight path. As they came within sight of the large glowing water planet, Tarikon, four war frigates sat in wait, ready to destroy the captured ship.

"Sir, we have four frigates at our prow stationed at ten, eleven, one and two o' clock!"

Before the captain and his men could react, a volley of fire poured from the four waiting warships' cannons, ripping into the shell of their own ship, shaking it like an earthquake. The captain and his men regained their composure, belting themselves down through the quaking chaos.

"Sir at this rate, we will break apart before we reach the atmosphere."

"Just concentrate on getting us close enough to fire that bomb."

While the four frigates were well armed, they were designed to destroy much smaller targets than that of a frigate and although they were doing colossal damage, it was not enough to stop such a substantial ship. Fire and smoke began to pour into the bridge as the damage on their ship mounted threatening to engulf them at any moment.

"Lieutenant, fire when in range," commanded the captain. "We can't miss on this one."

The lieutenant watched his target screen, tuning out the turmoil coming down around him, waiting for their super weapon to come within range of Tarikon's atmosphere. As soon as his screen flashed green, he punched the button without thinking firing it into space. The gigantic green ball launched into space, flying just below the four firing frigates before sinking into the huge glowing blue globe below. The volley of fire upon their ship continued, ironically forcing the large vessel out of orbit and into a collision course with the very planet they had come to destroy. The ship's captain sat back in a pile of rubble, smoke and fire as the ship around him began to crumble in upon him and sighed with a smile. As he soared toward his death, he had never felt such a complete feeling of satisfaction. He would die with no regrets and best of all with good men.

"Sir, we have been docked!" screamed his young officer over the destruction of their ship.

The captain rose up wondering why the phikogars would risk boarding a deteriorating ship. Then the phikogar he hated most came to mind, Baertuhjk! That slimy bastard hated humans so much that he had actually come aboard, risking his own life to finish them by his own hand! The captain jumped to his feet and pulled out his long knife, the death of his long despised phikogar counterpart was the only thing that could make this successful moment sweeter.

"Men," he commanded, "stand ready to engage the enemy!"

"Sir, it's the Barley Belly… she has docked at our stern!" he yelled in excitement.

Every man in the bridge cheered in exhilaration at the possibility of rescue, only Captain Armonil showed signs of displeasure toward the surprise news. They had risked too much for such a small likelihood of rescue. He would beat the shit out of Captain Duchey, he thought in anger.

"Sir, they have hailed us."

"Put them on!"

The large screen nearly the size of a full movie theater lit up showing Captain Duchey on the bridge with Felicity and the young eudaemonian officer at his side.

"What the hell do you think you doing?" screamed Captain Armonil.

"We came here to rescue our people!" replied the new captain.

"Do you realize what jeopardy you have put us all in by doing what you have done?"

"You have no say in this matter," interrupted Felicity. "Now get down here because we are not leaving without you."

The Captain looked at the huge screen in aggravation as his men stood ready to run or stand and die by his command.

"Lieutenant Eloi, set a course to go directly between those two center frigates," he said looking at his desperate men. "Well, what are you all waiting for? Let's get down there and save their assess!"

The men screamed with adrenaline as they dashed through the structure of the destructing ship, navigating through smoke, fire and wreckage along the way. Although angry at their defiance, Captain Armonil was glad to once again see the docking bay of the *Barley Belly* and the rest of his men awaiting their arrival. As the last man fell through the small ship's docking door, Captain Duchey ordered his bridge to break free and began what they hoped would be a successful escape. Upon breaking free of its hold upon the monster frigate, the ship's two captains stood eye to eye with no one certain of what form their greeting would take. Still angry, Captain Armonil punched Captain Duchey in the stomach causing him to collapse to the floor.

"Thank you captain," said Captain Armonil.

"Please, no more gratitude," he replied hunched over struggling to breathe. "Welcome back sir."

The large collapsing frigate set on a kamikaze course collided with the two desperately firing frigates, exploding into their structures and sending the three in a spiraling crash into the atmosphere of the large planet below. Behind the enormous collision, the small freight ship carrying the precious genetic material of human life once again escaped into the vast cosmos. As the small ship bore its way through the stars, a once beautiful bright blue planet changed to a smoke green, eliminating all forms of life on its surface.

# Cosmic Contemplations

With the death of billions of phikogars under their belts, the inhabitants of the *Barley Belly* engaged in a huge ship wide celebration that overwhelmed every member of the small ship. While the people of Earth celebrated the death of a planet, those of Eudaemonia rejoiced only for the lives that were saved. No one other than officers helped the captain with the preparation of the large meal that centered the festivity, as he was never personally happier than when he was preparing food. With the raid of the frigate ship, they had stocked both their food and fuel supplies to the max and with the home planet of the phikogars suffering the same fate as Earth, their future had never seemed so bright since the war had began. The captain and his culinary crew of officers wheeled the large meal into the main cargo hold, where for the first time, every member of the ship whether they were officer, soldier, worker or eudaemonian all shared each other's company. The celebration went on all night and while the next morning most slept in late with permission from their captain, Captain Armonil awoke bright and early to plot their course. A small knock at the door stole his attention from the charts on his desk.

"Please come in."

The thin graceful form of Felicity glided into his office.

"I guess I owe you my gratitude," he said humbly. "Mr. Duchey explained to me that you were the one that convinced him to come and rescue us."

"Yes," she said softly.

"Well, thank you," he said kindly.

"You are welcome. You know that is the first time you have ever said anything nice to me."

"Hmm… I guess I have never really been good at being nice. Even as a chef I had a bad temper, expected perfection," he said pondering the whole matter. "Let me ask you something. Why did you come back for us?"

"Captain, even though I do not understand your attraction to violence, I do appreciate life and as a eudaemonian, it is my duty to preserve it whenever possible."

He listened to her kind words, unsure what to say next, as most every word that had left his mouth since Earth had been in the form of an order. She sat down beside him and although she was a decade his elder, she held an exotic beauty that captured his eye. He

172

had not looked at a woman the way he looked at her since he last saw his wife alive on Earth. An uncontrollable urge overcame the two, pulling them together in a long passionate kiss. The door to his office swung open.

"Sir…" said the young officer stunned by the scene he had interrupted.

"What the hell are you doing coming in here without knocking?" the captain screamed at the young man.

"Sir, I am sorry, but we have received an open transmission from Baertuhjk," he said with a smirk on his face.

"Wipe that smile of your face right now soldier and I swear to you, if anyone hears of this, you will be on latrine duty until the day you die."

Felicity smiled at being caught like a little girl making out in her room.

"Yes sir!" the officer stated dropping his smile like a bad habit.

The captain got up and headed to the bridge with Felicity at his side. They stepped in to find Mr. Duchey alone in the bridge.

"Good morning sir, good morning Felicity," he said, greeting the two. "Sorry about sending Lieutenant Eloi, but I was sure you wanted to take this one personally."

The captain stood tall, straightening his clothes, "Go ahead and put him on."

The long screen flickered, revealing the enraged expressions of Baertuhjk.

"Good morning," hailed the captain.

"The pain of your deaths shall be tenfold for what you have done!" screamed the gray mass on screen.

"You and your people fucked up when you attacked Earth. Paybacks are hell!" he said coldly.

"You are a fool if you think this has helped you in your blight upon the universe!"

"What does Giouaal think about you now that the one ship you were assigned to destroy has destroyed the very planet he gave you as a homeland?"

"Do not speak his name you infidel!" it screamed wildly thrashing its arms.

"Did you have a wife and children there like I did on Earth?"

"Your acts shall never be forgotten nor will the pain of your death."

"Up till now, you have been coming for us, but now I am coming for you, Baertuhjk. Long live Jonkierdeat, the next father of the universe!"

Mr. Duchey cut transmission at his captain's command once again so not to the give the angered phikogar the last word. No one in the room believed in, or knew anything about a god named Jonkierdeat, especially Captain Armonil, but he delighted in dropping the name in front of his enemies. Felicity stood next to the captain. She would never understand his violent nature. But she did understand his loyalty to his people and she loved him for that.

# Death to the Queen

## "The invasion has begun"

# Cosmic Contemplations

# Part I
# The Invasion

---

Hundreds of thousands of ships orbited the vast desert planet, standing ready under the command of one man.

"Sir, all transports have been launched," reported the lieutenant. "The invasion has begun."

"Call off all ground strikes and scan drop sites Bravo, Charlie, and Delta," commanded General Luohond. "Make sure they are clear for landing."

A parade of "yes sirs" filled the bridge as General Luohond prepared to command the largest invasion in the history of mankind.

"Sir, our transports have broken the outer atmosphere," reported the lieutenant. "Estimated time of arrival is six minutes."

"Begin bombardment on target site Alpha and have divisions Bravo, Charlie, and Delta ready upon my command," ordered General Luohond.

The plan was simple. Divisions Bravo, Charlie, and Delta were to land at their respective sites and secure their positions. In the meanwhile, the galactic command would bombard attack point Alpha, protecting the landing troops from a possible counter attack by the enemy until they were ready for an all out assault. This planet was infested with the myloid race; a breed of highly developed, semi-intelligent arthropods that had been invading and consuming worlds for centuries. Several planets colonized by the United Galactic Systems had been overrun and annihilated by the myloids over the past several decades. The general had seen the myloids first hand as a young officer, finding them horrible creatures not worth spitting on in his professional opinion. A single one could easily dispatch five good men if it got close enough. Worst of all they bred twenty times the rate of humans and matured to adulthood in a single year. They moved from planet to planet inside spores that were somehow shot through the atmosphere. Once the spore reached a suitable host planet, the myloids would emerge quickly developing into adults and consume all life, including both plant and animal. Once all the available food sources were gone, their own cycle of life would end. How or when these spores were released was still a mystery.

General Luohond had been selected as the supreme commander over militaristic forces of the United Galactic Systems. His mission was to seek out and eliminate this little known race of parasitic beings. It was man's first all out assault on these creatures. In doing so, the general hoped to discover the secret to how the species spread through the cosmos.

"Sir divisions Bravo, Charlie, and Delta are in place," reported the lieutenant.

"Cease fire on target Alpha and have all forces ready to move on my command," said the stoic general. "Captain, I want a full scan and report on the status of target Alpha."

The captain took a few seconds to run a scan of movement and life around target Alpha and reported, "Sir, surface scan shows an enemy life count of 3.4 million. Movement is at a minimal."

"Lieutenant, give divisions Bravo, Charlie, and Delta the command to take and hold position Alpha. Captain, I want constant reports on both friendly and enemy life counts and movement throughout the assault," commanded the general.

"Sir, friendly life count is currently at 25.4 million. All major movements are friendly," reported the captain.

The general knew that taking position Alpha would be costly and causalities, even though they had a strategic and numerical advantage, were expected to reach as high as thirty percent. Once target Alpha was taken, all that remained would be to clean up the few remaining stragglers. The general's concentration was broken by the frayed voice of his captain.

"Sir, I am picking up a large concentration of enemy movement behind all three of our divisions!" yelled the captain.

The general leapt to his feet and ordered his lieutenant to

inform all divisions of the current situation.

The captain continued with his report, "Currently, friendly life count is at 25.4 and enemy is at 12.5. Enemy movement is closing in on all three divisions."

"I want every division to stop their advance and prepare for an all out rear assault!" screamed the general.

"Sir," reported the lieutenant, "our units are reporting heavy contact with the enemy."

The general began to pace the bridge, evaluating his every available strategic option. Air strikes on his men would be a last resort. New reinforcements wouldn't have a suitable place to land and a full withdrawal or retreat wasn't possible. Their only hope was that his men could fight it out.

"Sir, enemy movement and life count is growing. Current enemy life count is 22.9 and friendly is at 21.7," announced the captain.

"Lieutenant, find out where their reinforcements are coming from! Then call immediate missile fire on those coordinates," screamed the general in frustration.

The general couldn't understand it. They had orbited and surveyed this planet for over a month and the enemy's life count had never topped 4 million. Now, all of a sudden, myloids were swarming out of nowhere.

"Sir, enemy life count is 27.3 and friendly is 17.5," announced the captain once again.

"Lieutenant, prepare transport divisions Kilo, Lima, and Mike for launch!" ordered the alarmed general. "Where is my missile fire?"

"Sir," reported the lieutenant looking up from his screen, "missile control cannot get a lock on the enemies' origin."

"I don't give a shit!" declared the general at a deafening tone. "Tell them to fire at something before there is nothing left to support!"

"Sir, enemy life count is now 32.3 and friendly life is 12.8," said the captain.

"Sir, all missile strikes have been launched," reported the lieutenant.

Every man on the bridge anxiously waited in silence for the results of the missile report. The general paced the length of his bridge, afraid to ask for a report that would spell the success or failure of his mission. After several long intense moments, the lieutenant spoke.

"Sir, our missiles have made a direct hit!" he declared.

The men of the bridge erupted in cheer.

"Scramble all transports for pick up!" ordered the general.

"All transports from divisions Kilo, Lima and Mike have been dispatched. Estimated time of arrival is 3 minutes," reported the lieutenant.

"Captain, status report," commanded the general.

"Enemy life count is 25.2 and stationary and friendly is currently stable at 9.6," answered the captain.

"Get down there," said the general, under his breath.

"Landing time is two minutes and counting sir," reported the lieutenant again.

"Sir," bellowed the captain in distress, "we have enemy movement!"

"I want constant missile strikes on all previously hit coordinates, until I say otherwise!" ordered the general.

"Enemy life count is 29.7 and friendly is 8.8," reported the captain.

"Landing time is 1.5 minutes and counting," reported the lieutenant.

The general stood helplessly. He had done everything in his power and it had not been enough. All he could do was listen to the reports of his subordinates.

"Enemy life count is 35.9 and friendly is 2.1!" reported the captain.

"Estimated landing time is one minute and counting," announced the lieutenant.

"Sir," the captain said dishearteningly, "friendly life count is zero."

Silence followed those words and not a breath was taken. The general fell back into his chair and put his face into his hands.

"Call back the transports and stop all missile strikes," he cried, mumbling through his hands. "It's over."

And just like that, twenty-five and a half million men died, or so the U.G.S. command thought.

# Part II
# The Surface

---

Corporal Hendricks' squad, which was part of Division Bravo, had been part of the right wing, which was to encircle position Alpha and cut off any possible retreat once it was hit by the spearhead of Division Delta. They had been hit hard and were overrun by the enemy when the missile strikes began. The corpse of an enemy myloid and the side of a dune had shielded his body saving his life. Pushing the tough exoskeleton of a burnt myloid off his leg, Corporal Hendricks surveyed the scene of death before his eyes. The burnt flesh of both friend and foe filled the cavities of his lungs, while the cries of his fellow men became the theme song of this new war. The intense heat caused by the blast had burned the flesh of his fellow troops to a crisp, but it had a different effect on their enemy. The myloids appeared to be more sensitive to heat and it had affected even those who had been shielded from the blast. It shrunk their exoskeleton, immobilizing their shells to the point of useless wiggling. Avoiding the shriveled bodies of his enemy, Corporal Hendricks began to search for survivors. The missile strikes had done their job in stopping the counterstrike and he wondered if the rest of the marines had succeeded in taking position Alpha. He looked up at the sky, almost expecting to see reinforcements, but the sky was clear, not even a cloud for a rescue pod to hover behind. The heat from the glass fragments below his feet intensified the temperature of the surrounding desert searing his burnt skin. He followed the cries for help, but found only men who were beyond saving. Most of them were burnt beyond recognition and were nothing more than black bundles of distorted crying flesh. Others had been torn apart from the blast, but the heat of the ensuing waves had sealed up their wounds and stopped them from bleeding, allowing the poor souls to suffer a little longer. He sighed as tears began to form in his eyes. He had hoped to find Private Brandell, whom he had been best friends with since basic. They had sat side by side during the landings, but had been separated during the intense battle that followed. For all he knew, he had already found him, but was unable to recognize him. As he had almost given up hope, a distant voice called out to him.

"Hey!" it paused for a moment. "Hey you, up here!" it said.

Corporal Hendricks looked up to see a small dune to the right of his position. On top of the dune loomed the silhouette of a soldier under the blazing sun. His hair was very short, keeping in tradition with the older soldiers and bright white. The man motioned his arms, signaling for Corporal Hendricks to come up and then disappeared behind the dune. Corporal Hendricks hoisted his heavy rifle onto his shoulders and began to ascend the dune on which the man had been standing. Upon reaching the top, he found the edge of the hill housed a depression with a crater like shape. Inside the crater sat a platoon of men. They showed no signs of exposure to the immense blasts of the counterstrikes ordered from above. Their skin showed no signs of burns, such as his, and even their flak vests were still covered in cloth. There were nine of them in all and most importantly, their equipment hadn't been damaged. One of the men was trying to make a transmission to galactic control.

"Galactic Control, this is wun tree six over..." he said waiting, "I say again... Galactic Control, this is wun tree six over..." he repeated.

"We've been trying to hail them for twenty minutes, but nobody is answering," said the man who had waved him in.

"Do you have any idea how the rest of the invasion went?" asked Corporal Hendricks.

"We've been in this hole since the assault by those fucking things out there," he said. "You probably have a better idea of what is going on around here than us."

"Yeah," replied Corporal Hendricks unemotionally.

"Shit, more of them!" cried another one of the men.

Corporal Hendricks and Sergeant Yap grabbed their rifles, ran and fell at the rim of their protective dune. Hundreds of myloids began to pour from holes in the ground. The myloids immediately began attacking the hundreds of wounded soldiers that littered the area around the circular dune. The aliens had long spike-like pinchers on their head, were longer than tall, being about four feet tall and nearly seven feet long, and walked on six legs. They moved along the ground much like ants and attacked the poor surviving souls of the blast in groups much the same way ants protect a mound. The ten men lay in silence and watched the horror before them down the barrels of their rifles.

Eventually, the inevitable happened and myloids began to search with their tentacles along the base of their dune where the soldiers were hidden. Sergeant Yap gave the order to fire and initially the defenders, using their natural fortress to create enfilade, held strong. But the myloids began to get closer to the rim of the soldier's defense with each wave of attack. Once they were over the rim, it would be a slaughter. Sergeant Yap gave the order for a slow pull out and Private Maus went over the backside of the dune with a flamethrower. Sergeant Yap ordered two more men to go as his wingmen and Private Maus began to clear a path for their withdrawal to a small hole barely forty meters away. The heat of the flames from his thrower shrunk the exterior of the myloids unfortunate enough to get within its range and held back the attack. Corporal Hendricks continued to hold back the rear as his new platoon switched fronts. The myloids swarmed over into the soldier's depression as a well placed grenade by Sergeant Yap obliterated their advance. The men's slow withdrawal turned into a full retreat once they left the safety of their defensive hole. Fighting for their lives, the small squad reached the outside of their destination with the loss of only two men. The constant flames of Private Maus held the multitude of myloids at bay, while Sergeant Yap cleared the hole with a grenade.

"Go, Go, Go!" hollered Sergeant Yap, pointing into the hole bellowing smoke.

All of the men filed inside, while Private Maus stood outside holding off the myloid assault.

"Private Buckley, get me an energy gate ready to go!" screamed the sergeant.

Private Buckley pulled out a roll of metallic tape and began to tape a circle around the entrance to the tunnel.

"You two go ahead and hold our perimeter," ordered the sergeant pointing into the black hole.

Once Private Buckley had set up the dimensions of the energy gate, he sat a charger at its base and the sergeant ordered Private Maus in, but before he could do so, a myloid seized the retreating soldier. It shredded the poor man in seconds, puncturing one of his flamethrower tanks, causing an explosion that tore into the hole burning everything within a ten foot radius. Private Buckley was killed while waiting to set the energy gate nearly evaporating in the heat of the explosion. Quickly, Corporal Hendricks dove to the energy wall's charger and flipped the switch. A thick blue wall of energy instantly sprang up to stop the onrush of myloids. One myloid was killed as the beam of pure energy cut through the creature slicing it cleanly in half as it leaped over the tape at the moment of the wall's activation. The wall stretched across the entire entrance to the tunnel and was as thick as the tape placed by the late private Buckley. It was at the moment, all that saved the men from utter destruction

"We have about two hours before the battery dies down," said the sergeant in charge. "Let's see where this thing leads."

# Part III
# Underground

---

The six remaining men of Division Bravo began their march into the surface's crust, distancing themselves from their seemingly limitless enemy. Corporal Hendricks had taken Private Buckely's gear and after finding it in good condition, was placed in charge of it by Sergeant Yap. In all, he found three more energy batteries and two more rolls of metallic tape in his possession. They had lost their best offensive weapon with the death of Private Maus and the destruction of the flamethrower, so it was the decision of Sergeant Yap that they should switch from fragmentary to incendiary rounds.

They marched slowly under the command of Sergeant Yap, fearful of running into their enemy and kept both front and rear guards. Hidden from the suns of Nemhunic, the tunnels would have engulfed the poor men in darkness were it not for the lights beneath the barrels of their guns. The tunnels themselves were only about five feet tall, making their march long and arduous, and from the marks along the walls, appeared to have been recently dug by their myloid foes. Every time one of their helmets inadvertently scraped the ceiling, loose soil gave away and covered them in a cloud of dust, making breathing a labor and restricting their sight.

They continued on for three hours before Sergeant Yap gave them orders to stop and rest. Corporal Hendricks took off his backpack and fell back against the wall. His back ached immensely from carrying his heavy gear while hunched over to avoid the low ceiling of the myloid's tunnel. A soldier took a cigarette out to light, but only succeeded in having it slapped out of his mouth by Sergeant Yap.

"What the fuck do you think you're doing? We're trying to get away from these things and you're leaving them smoke signals!" he said looking at the man agitated. "All right everybody listen up! We've got to pick up the pace a little. According to Corporal Hendricks, we only have three chargers left and once those are gone, I believe it's safe to say so are we. So this is going to be our last stop! If you have to piss you better do it now, because the next time you'll have to do it while on the run. Let's move out!" he yelled standing up.

Corporal Hendricks liked the crusty old sergeant that stood before him with his thick white mustache that bounced around on his lip as he barked his orders. His methods may have been a little crude, but he kept them organized and focused.

Carrying the majority of the equipment, Corporal Hendricks had been commanded to bring up the rear. The darkness that followed behind him made him feel uneasy and it seemed that the men in front couldn't move fast enough for him to escape its dark grip. Several of the men wanted to go ahead and set up a new energy barrier to stop a possible advance from the rear, but Sergeant Yap wisely refused, knowing that every second they waited, was another second that they had to get out alive.

Having no choice but to follow the direction dictated by the tunnel, the soldiers continued to march deeper into the crust of Nemhunic, further from their distant mothership hovering beyond its thin atmosphere. Whether they actually had a chance or if this forced march was only postponing the inevitable, Sergeant Yap wasn't sure. All he knew was that they were following the only possible chance they had. On the surface, they would eventually be overwhelmed no matter how good of a defensive position they held. At least here, they could hide, but for how long he wasn't sure.

The simplicity of their predicament became far more complicated when they arrived at a three-way junction. Two tunnels, the one from whence they came and the one to their left, slanted upward as if to go back toward the surface, while the third sloped down toward the planet's core. Making a snap decision so as not to waste valuable time, Sergeant Yap decided that it would be best to stay as close to the surface as possible and chose to take the new tunnel that had a gradient sloping toward the surface. If the other divisions had fared better, they could conceivably emerge in friendly territory.

This new turn of circumstances did much for the spirit of their small group and a couple of the men smiled as they began to hike up toward the surface. Corporal Hendricks began to feel that under the quick and able command of Sergeant Yap, they stood a chance even against odds as great as their own. He began to wonder if it would be night or day when they reached the surface when the cracking voice of the point guard broke his concentration.

"Here they come!" he screamed in a rush of adrenaline.

"Hold your position!" ordered the commanding sergeant.

Fire poured from the barrels of the men's guns wiping out the first wave of attackers. Only a few seconds passed before a second wave of myloids swarmed over the bodies of the first and almost breached the soldiers' small front line. One of the myloids got hold of Private Kubley before the creature was ripped open by an incendiary round. Corporal Hendricks pulled the wounded soldier to the rear and tried to stop the flow of blood pouring from the wounded man's chest. The wound, which started on one side of the soldier's chest, traveled completely across his thoracic cavity, exposing the organs of both his pleural cavities and his pericardial cavity. The wound was about a full inch deep and before Corporal Hendricks could do anything, he was holding the body of a dead man.

Unable to see through the smoke and dust of their surroundings, Sergeant Yap called for a slow withdrawal toward the three-way junction they had passed earlier. The tunnel was barely wide enough for three men to stand side by side, but that is what they did as they gradually gave ground. For every myloid a round split apart, another would emerge through the dust to replace it. By the time they reached the junction, the barrels of their rifles had turned white from the heat of repeated firing.

Sergeant Yap ordered Corporal Hendricks to set up an energy barrier at the mouth of the tunnel leading down further into the earth. Hurriedly, Corporal Hendricks pulled out his tape and began to apply it around the tunnel wall as quickly as he could without compromising the connection the energy barrier would need to hold an energy flux. Then he sat a charger at its base and yelled that it was ready. He sat ready and watched as his fellow soldiers began to pull toward him.

Without the confinements of the tunnel, myloids began to pour out into the large three-way junction. The men began to fire in all directions shooting at the floor, walls and ceiling. Two myloids managed to avoid the stream of fire coming from the small group of men, compromised their ranks and engaged the men in hand to hand combat. Alertly using his energy sword, Sergeant Yap gutted one myloid from its neck to its torso. As he did so, another dropped from the ceiling and tore him apart in a fury beyond any Corporal Hendricks had ever seen. Dozens of myloids swarmed upon the dead sergeant, giving the four remaining soldiers a chance to retreat.

The myloids pursued with the speed of lightning and even though his finger sat on the switch itself, Corporal Hendricks barely managed to flip it in time. A thick shield of bright blue energy burst forth and occupied the area between the two armies. Once again they had defied the will of death.

# Part IV
# The Queen

---

Corporal Hendricks' hair still stood on end, even after they were well beyond the force of their last energy barrier. The four remaining men, who had been in good spirits just a few minutes earlier, now shuffled through the dark tunnel completely demoralized, their hopes taken away with the loss of their sergeant. The sergeant's cool demeanor and indubitable leadership had assembled them into a unit instead of a group of individuals and inspired them to move on even when it seemed hopeless.

Now reality sunk in and in their own minds they were as good as dead, it was merely a question of how long before death came calling for the last time. The rabble of men were nearly out of projectile ammo, both incendiary and fragmentary and would eventually have to switch to the use of heat lasers, which they had discovered during the main invasion did not always penetrate the rough exoskeleton of their enemies, especially at long range.

The slope of the tunnel became steeper with each step and eventually they had to shoulder their weapons and use their hands to keep balance. The long oval monotonous underground passage finally came to an end and dropped into a lower chamber. Corporal Hendricks, who had continued to bring up the rear of their squad, was the last to drop into the chamber with his fellow men.

It was pitch dark and the small lights of their rifles did little to illuminate their new surroundings. They began to scan around the walls with their lights, but found that the small lights weren't strong enough to penetrate the thick darkness of the myloid's underground labyrinth. Fumbling through his gear, Private Foster pulled a flare from his pack and struck it along the wall. A burst of bright red light engulfed the group and for several seconds none of the men could see a thing, save rings of light that had imbedded themselves into their vision. Once their eyes adjusted, the four stood stunned.

Before them was a chamber, nearly two hundred feet in length covered in shifting white larvae. Myloids similar to the ones that had fought on the surface, but with smaller frames and pinchers, were taking hold of the larvae and pulling them into holes that littered the opposite walls. They had stumbled into some type of breeding chamber.

Corporal Hendricks was the first to discharge his weapon and a volley of rounds followed from the rest of the men. The new, smaller myloids fell quickly and in minutes the men had slain everything within sight. Thick white puss bubbled from the soft bodies of the dead and dying larvae.

Corporal Hendricks' mind suddenly clicked. It all made sense. These myloids were part of a complex social organization, much like that of common ants or bees. The larger myloids they had fought on the surface were the warriors, while the smaller ones they had just encountered tending to the young, were the workers. Site Alpha was nothing more than a giant anthill and they were in the middle of it.

"Hurry up! Let's get into one of these tunnels, before they catch us out in the open," ordered Corporal Hendricks.

He began to walk across the giant chamber toward the numerous tunnel entrances along the adjacent wall when a voice hailed him to stop.

"When the hell were you put in charge?" it asked.

Corporal Hendricks turned around to see his challenger, Corporal Crager, standing in defiance of his newly taken command.

"What would you suggest we do?" replied Hendricks.

"I think we should turn back and try to make it to the surface. At least that way we might be rescued!" he answered.

"The only thing you are going to find that way is more of those big fucking bugs that tore Sergeant Yap apart like a wet paper doll! We don't stand a chance that way," said Corporal Hendricks.

"And you think going further down is going to save us?" Corporal Crager yelled in response.

# Death to the Queen

"Look," said Corporal Hendricks calmly, "these things are separated in castes, all with specific duties. The ones we have temporarily sealed off behind us are the warriors, while the ones we just sent crawling below are workers and if my theory is right that means that they probably have a queen. If we can manage to kill her, then we manage to kill the whole colony. The way I look at it, I would rather chase those workers who just ran from us than to tangle with those warriors who have been running us."

"Well God damn! We've got ourselves an insect expert on our hands!" Corporal Crager mocked.

Corporal Hendricks pointed his gun at the mutinous soldier, startling him, causing him to jerk up his own gun in defense.

"What is the date of your rank soldier?" asked Hendricks boldly.

"August '34," was the nervous reply.

"Then the problem is solved. I out rank you by two months," said Hendricks.

"You're not even from this platoon! How the hell do I know you are telling the truth?" Corporal Crager asked, wiping a bead of sweat from his forehead.

"My right to command this squad has been established," Corporal Hendricks said firmly, "any further resistance will be considered insubordination. So I suggest that you lower your gun before I separate you from it!"

A moment of trepidation passed over the small group as the two corporals stood motionless, staring each other down. Not a move was made by any of the men, until Corporal Crager lowered his gun bringing the four men to sighs of relief. Corporal Hendricks had settled the conflict between his own men, but now a far more difficult task lay ahead.

"Stop gawking and start walking," commanded Corporal Hendricks, "and load up, we're going down below to get the rest of them."

The men chose a random hole and began their journey, searching for a creature that might or might not exist. They met slight resistance from worker myloids, but these myloids didn't have aggressive or efficient attack formations, as did the warriors. The four soldiers had little trouble dispatching the creatures. They hadn't encountered any warriors since the loss of Sergeant Yap and Corporal

Hendricks hoped that maybe they had somehow trapped the warrior myloids above for the time being.

Having no way of finding their target, save blind luck, the men moved as quickly as they could from one chamber to the next, stopping only to eradicate the larvae of two more breeding chambers. The deeper they went, the larger the tunnels became and the easier it was for them to move freely. The tunnels eventually grew so large in size that they were able to stand up completely.

As soon as things seemed to be going their way, their luck ran out. They were chasing a small group of worker myloids that were attempting to save some larvae, when the tunnel began to rumble horribly. Corporal Hendricks gave them the signal to stop and listen. Dirt began to fall all around their position, making the air was so thick with dust that it became nearly impossible to see or breathe.

"It sounds like it's coming from all around us," said Private Green coughing.

"They're digging through!" cried Corporal Crager.

Those words had hardly left his mouth when warrior myloids bore through the tunnel's walls. Myloids poured into the tunnel, cutting off Private Foster from the rest of the group devouring him. The soldier's barrels went to work and repealed the first onslaught, giving the men time to retreat. They ran straight until they found themselves in another large chamber.

Corporal Hendricks grabbed his last roll of metallic tape and began to tape up the entrance to their new chamber. Corporal Crager stood ahead, covering him until he was ready to flip the switch. Another barrier jumped up between the three men and their enemy. Once again they had successfully delayed certain death.

In the darkness of the new chamber, the three men focused their eyes, using the light from their energy barrier to see what lay ahead. They were able to see about twenty some odd feet ahead and at first, the chamber appeared to be empty. As he attempted to light a flare, something seized Corporal Crager and pulled him into the darkness. Corporal Hendricks and Private Green opened fire, creating flashes of light that illuminated their enemies swarming toward their position in an illusion that made them appear to be in slow motion. Worker and warrior myloids attempted to reach the frantically firing men forcing their backs against their own energy field. A worker got a grip on Corporal Hendricks' leg and ripped both his armor and flesh.

# Death to the Queen

A clean shot to its mesothorax split it wide open and caused its claws to slide painfully off his leg. In intense pain, Corporal Hendricks fell to one knee and continued to fire. Then like a bolt of lightning, the attack stopped altogether and nothing could be seen or heard, aside from the buzz emitted by their energy field. Cautiously, Private Green struck a flare bringing light to the enormous chamber. Huddled in the middle, blinded by the great light, was the immense and vulnerable queen. She was a full twenty feet in length and as big as an anthropic elephant. Severely wounded and unable to move, she lay quivering. The two remaining soldiers fired their remaining rounds, leaving themselves defenseless, but victorious. The shots of Corporal Hendricks and Private Green put the queen out of her misery and redeemed the deaths of nearly twenty five and a half million men.

# Intergalactic Dimensions

In the farthest stretches of the cosmos lie rocks and fire
Swirling and burning since the beginning of time
Expanding upon themselves and extending into nothing
Consuming, conflicting and overshadowing one another
Sometimes to create and nourish life
Other times to merely degenerate
Or even bring it to full circle and hence completion
It is the way of chaos,
The loss of one means only the eventual beginning of another
And therefore ensuring everlasting life

# Other stories available from Portal Press

**Autobiography of a Necromancer**, By Charles Clemons. Synopsis: An anonymous necromancer chronicles his life, including both his successes and failures as a resurrecter of the dead. ($5.00), Short Story, Pamphlet.

**King of the Hunt**, By Charles Clemons. Synopsis: A king and legendary hunter, becomes locked in a battle of survival against a brutal beast. ($4.00), Short Story, Pamphlet.

**The Quest Knights**, By Charles Clemons. Synopsis: Four knights are sent on a quest to save their kingdom. ($3.00), Short Story, Pamphlet.

**Primordial Beast,** By Charles Clemons. Synopsis: A man contracts a virus that awakens ancient memories and desires that conflict with today's civilization. ($4.00), Short Story, Pamphlet.

**The Desert a Few Deceptions and Some Dough,** By Charles Clemons. Synopsis: Throw in four people, a pinch of dough, a side of Las Vegas, a dash of greed, and serve in the desert and you have a recipe for a good story. ($5.00), Short Story, Pamphlet.

**Satan's Side of the Story: An Interview,** By Charles Clemons. Synopsis: In an interview Satan is allowed to tell his side of the first story ever told. ($7.00), Interview, Pamphlet, includes a CD recording.

There are now two ways to get high quality strange fiction from Portal Press:

## Snail Mail

Please send a letter detailing the items for purchase and check or money order for the total amount of purchase plus $3.00 shipping and handling for up to three pamphlets (add .50 cents for each one beyond the third) to:

Portal Press
9706 Ricole Trail
Soddy Daisy, TN 37379

Please allow up to three weeks for delivery.

## Online

Our entire inventory is available at:

www.portalpressbooks.com.

Please allow up to two weeks for delivery.

Portal Press
www.portalpressbooks.com